The regulation cotton dress Alison had on underneath clung damply and all too revealingly to her body. Steve leaned an elbow on the wall above her and looked down. Suddenly he was no longer the detached surgeon. He was all man. And he was too close—alarmingly close.

'Allow me.' He pulled the tight cap from her head, releasing her hair in a cloud about her shoulders. 'Is that better?' His hair was tousled, his blue eyes baiting her with good humour, he was laughing down at her. Was it any wonder women found him irresistible? Alison wondered, hot and flustered and nervously brushing a curtain of silk from her cheeks.

'Now tell me, what's so important you can't make it tomorrow?' His voice had an unfamiliar softness, and he was still far, far too close . . .

Polly Beardsley returned to her native New Zealand to begin her training as a nurse, after raising a family and many years travelling with a husband whose medical career took them to live in England, the USA, and the Far East. On graduating from Nursing School, Polly worked in a busy surgical ward as Staff Nurse and then in the operating theatre, before coming back to London to work in an inner city hospital. Her first Doctor-Nurse romance, *On Call in Theatre*, was published last year.

NEW ZEALAND NURSE

BY

POLLY BEARDSLEY

MILLS & BOON LIMITED
ETON HOUSE 18-24 PARADISE ROAD
RICHMOND SURREY TW9 1SR

First published in Great Britain 1988
by Mills & Boon Limited

© Polly Beardsley 1988

Australian copyright 1988
Philippine copyright 1988
This edition 1988

ISBN 0 263 76149 5

Set in Plantin 10 on 10 pt.
03 – 0888 – 62236

Typeset in Great Britain by JCL Graphics, Bristol

Made and printed in Great Britain

CHAPTER ONE

'IF SHE'S anything like her father . . .' Steve Barratt, Paediatric Registrar at Fort William Hospital, broke off to take a disgruntled swipe with his tennis racquet at a hovering wasp. He missed, but as the pest flew away, he couldn't help but wish that Alison Prentice, the English Sister who had taken charge of the children's ward during his three weeks' holiday, was as easy to dispatch. He'd been dead against her appointment from the beginning, suspecting she was bound to be all the things he detested in a woman—hyper-efficient, opinionated, bossy even. And now that she had invaded his domain, he didn't much care to spend the last few hours of his precious leave discussing her. He glanced narrowly at the junior house surgeon standing by his side on his front lawn.

'She's very proper, everything gets done by the book,' Stuart Dalgleish had to admit—though the young doctor couldn't help a sneaking admiration for the way their new Sister was running the ward.

'I'll bet.' Steve's smile was grim. 'She comes from a London hospital renowned for old school formality—the bastion of English traditional nursing—or so it was when I was there.' Steve Barratt rarely if ever talked about his post-graduate years in England, and Stuart's interest quickened, as he had heard that he had done brilliantly well, coming home as the youngest Registrar ever to be appointed by the hospital.

'Her old man was a consultant there when I knew him. He runs an outfit that would put the Marines to shame, his housemen refer to him as the Iron Duke.' Steve rapped his leg with the racquet, 'And from what I've heard, his daughter takes after him. Cripes, who'd have thought she would turn up in a small New Zealand town.' He snorted. 'Though at her age—twenty-nine, isn't it—one could guess she's out here looking for a husband.'

5

'Wouldn't have thought she was twenty-nine,' Stuart murmured, surprised. 'Pretty nice little figure,' he added, sounding suspiciously defensive.

'Hmmm . . .' Steve ran a bemused eye over the house surgeon's button-down collar and tie. Hospital rules permitted the wearing of open-necked shirts, walking shorts and sandals during the hot summer months—why then was young Stuart sweltering in long serge trousers and brogues? His breath escaped in a whistle. The good Sister hadn't been wasting her time, apparently. Who knew what changes she might not have made while he had been away. He half expected he would find the nurses in starched petticoats. And this, during his campaign to get rid of uniforms altogether from the children's ward.

'Did you come over to discuss Sister's figure, or is there anything else?' he asked acidly.

Stuart shifted uneasily in his heavy leather shoes, feeling a little foolish disturbing Steve while he was still on leave. 'We're a bit concerned about this little kiddy we got in. She has a history of 'flu symptoms, high temperature, sore throat . . .'

'Rob McKenzie's on duty, isn't he?' Steve broke in, referring to the senior houseman.

'He doesn't think there's any need to worry,' Stuart mumbled, beginning to look acutely embarrassed.

'And Sister Prentice does. That it?' Steve demanded, a glint in his blue eyes. He knew the type—the Sister who made her own diagnosis and is never happy with the junior medical staff's opinions. Well, Rob might not look any great shakes, but he was perfectly competent at his job. And if a second opinion was wanted, why didn't Stuart call out Gilbert Hains? Then he remembered the consultant paediatrician was on one of his deep-sea fishing trips. He gave his racquet a regretful thwack; it looked as though his holiday was over.

'Well, OK, give me the details and I'll drop by the hospital and take a look-see.' He grinned suddenly. 'Soon as I let Clair know tennis is off for the afternoon.'

Watching Stuart reverse out of his drive, Steve chewed at the inner corner of his lip. Clair wouldn't be any too pleased he was going in to the hospital, she'd been looking forward to their game of tennis and it was her last day on holiday as well. He wondered how she would settle back on the ward under a new Sister, after having been acting charge for so long. Damned shame she hadn't got the job.

An hour later he turned into the entrance of the children's ward and looked warily about. The place looked the same—children in outsize dressing gowns and slippers pulling their mums to the playroom to show off a favourite toy, nurses dashing about in their ridiculous caps. That hadn't changed.

He walked along the corridor to Sister's office, glancing through the side room windows on the way. 'Hello,' he said softly, recognising a neighbour's child. Smiling, he went in, his eyes going automatically in a swift glance to the intravenous bottle overhead. Instantly he knew the drip was running at a dangerously high speed for so small a patient. Adjusting the rate immediately, he was still standing with the line in one hand when a clear, cool voice came from the doorway.

'Please don't interfere with the intravenous equipment.' Steve turned his head and saw a straight little figure in a severe white uniform, hair pulled uncompromisingly from a high forehead and pinned under a stiff starched veil. The eyes under the straight brows were as cool as her voice.

The office phone gave its strident ring and Alison Prentice paused on the threshold; that would be Casualty ringing about the baby with croup they were expecting. As the ringing continued, her lips tightened. The staff here seemed to think answering the phone was Sister's duty, whether she was in her office or not. The annoyance she felt showed in her face, though her voice was gentle—for the benefit of her young patient rather than this person who was fiddling with the drip, whoever he was. The child's uncle, family friend, whoever.

She stepped briskly forward with a soothing word to re-position the child's arm and tuck a teddy under the other; had checked the drip rate in one quick glance and swept from the room to disappear from sight, while Steve Barratt was still gazing furiously after her. If there was anything he detested more than an overly efficient woman, it was a brisk, uptight, overly efficient woman.

In her office, Alison snatched up the receiver, cradled it on her shoulder and reached for a pad. 'Kiri Mata,' she wrote, 'age three and a half, acute obstructive laryngitis . . . Right, I've got that. Thanks.' Looking up, she called to a passing staff nurse, and Jenny Duncan executed a smart U-turn in the corridor. Alison sighed with relief when the staff nurse's goodnatured face appeared at the doorway. She could rely on Jenny, and thank heaven for that.

'Can you prepare an oxygen tent, please, Jenny. We have a three-year-old with croup on the way.' She paused, a worried line between the elegant brows. 'Though maybe, if she's on the small side, as some Maori babies are, the croupette might be best.'

'I'll see to it,' Jenny said cheerfully, taking the notes Alison had jotted down. 'No problem.'

'Thanks,' Alison said, grateful she had someone with Jenny's experience, because when the case involved a small child in respiratory distress, experience counted more than anything.

Once again the phone started its persistent ringing and she automatically put a hand out to answer it. As she was speaking, Steve Barratt strolled into the office. 'Excuse me, please,' Alison murmured to the person on the other end of the line, and put a hand over the mouth piece.

'Would you mind waiting outside, please. I'll be with you in a moment,' she said; politely, but with an underlying bite of authority that let Steve know that she was used to getting her own way—and how, he thought.

Momentarily Alison paused. There was something unsettling about this tall, athletic-looking young man, with his insolent eyes. When she had a moment, she must check what his business was in the ward. She couldn't have just anybody wandering about, as people seemed to think they could do here. She was confident he would do as she requested, however, and turned away to resume her telephone conversation. It took her not very long to realise the stranger had not obeyed her instructions. Nettled, she cut short what she was saying and replaced the receiver with deliberation, before turning her cool eyes on him.

Steve took a seat on the edge of the desk, enjoying her look of shock, and nonchalantly swung a long tanned leg. 'Busy day, Sister?' He glanced at her, his sleepy-eyed manner changing so swiftly, Alison wondered if she had imagined it. 'I'm Steve Barratt. I heard you were in trouble, so I came to offer my help.'

'You're the Registrar?' Steve watched with amusement as her puzzled expression turned to embarrassment and then finally to horror. Alison had expected—well, she hadn't known what, exactly, but someone older, more professional-looking. Not this person with his leonine head of blond curls no man had any right to. Her eyes roved in disapproval over tennis shorts that seemed inadequate for so muscular a body, and came sharply up to the face, with its strong, confident features and heavy-lidded eyes.

She had a profound wish to drop into her chair, but she stood very still, regarding him gravely. 'That was kind of you,' she spoke carefully and precisely, 'but I wasn't aware we were in trouble—not enough, anyway, for you to curtail your leave . . . Mr Barratt.'

Steve's generous top lip curled slightly at the stinging rebuke given his name. 'No?' he drawled, mocking her. 'That little kid in room three would be awash by now, if I hadn't slowed up his IV.'

'But I checked it myself . . .'

'Only after I turned it back. Ever think of using an Ivac pump to regulate the rate? It would be a lot safer.'

His cocksure manner made her angry and she glared at him with distaste. 'We had three, and every one was malfunctioning. I sent them along to the engineers and they haven't come back yet. The state of the equipment in this ward is deplorable,' she snapped.

'I see . . . So it's the poor equipment,' he taunted, and watched a flush spread over her milky skin with an interest he couldn't quite contain. He knew her age, yet she looked far younger, and much prettier than he'd imagined. Obviously she didn't believe in wearing make-up on duty, even so, nothing could hide the long curling lashes and dark shapely brows—curious on one so fair—or the delicate bone structure and slender vulnerable neck. He had already noticed her legs: strong, clean, with trim ankles. Surprising she hadn't married.

Steve cleared his throat and got to his feet in one graceful movement. 'So you don't need my help.' He paused, waiting for her to speak.

'Ah . . .' Alison bit her lip under his slit-eyed regard. She hated the way he looked down his nose at her, as if she were a meal set out for him that didn't quite come up to scratch. Very well. Alison tilted her chin. Its determined line, a certain haughtiness in the greyish-green eyes, froze Steve on the spot. She was her father's daughter all right.

'I'm worried about a patient.' Alison's voice, although frostily polite, somehow managed to convey an expectation that she didn't have much faith in his ability to lessen it. 'And as you're here . . .'

'Lead the way, Sister.' Steve doffed an imaginary cap.

'You can save the theatricals for later,' Alison said, 'when you have a more appreciative audience.' It was the kind of comment she would have done best keeping to herself. But it had slipped out, and by the look on his face she knew she had made an enemy. Damn it. When she had so much wanted to be on good terms with the man who was tipped to take over Gilbert Hains's position when the consultant retired. But who could get along with this brash young man?

'This is Emma. She came in last night with a high temperature and sore throat, and since has become increasingly irritable and restless.' Alison bent over the bed. 'Hi, anyone in there? Doctor's come to say hello to you,' and she smiled, as a tousled head began to emerge from the blankets. It was a singularly sweet smile. She certainly didn't remind him of her father when she smiled, Steve thought, distracted.

'Sister tells me you're going to have your sixth birthday soon,' he said, when the little girl had been coaxed out. He sat down on the bed beside her. Alison had insisted that he wear a white coat, so with a wide grin, he fished enticingly into its pockets, bringing something out with great furtiveness.

Not only did he gain Emma's rapt attention, but Alison

found she was craning her own neck to see what might be in his closed fist. And when a clown's head popped out she gave an involuntary exclamation of delight, and immediately felt foolish, for Emma seemed less than impressed and was crossly trying to slide beneath her blankets again.

'Emma, look at me, please.' Steve took her small face in his large hands and studied it intently. 'Are your eyes hurting, is that why you like hiding under the blankets?'

The child nodded, and Steve gently set about a full and thorough examination. When he had finished, Alison followed him out to the wash-hand basin. 'What is your diagnosis, Sister?' he asked, soaping his hands, his glance at her swift, almost conspiratorial, for he knew full well she had one, and he was interested to know if they had arrived at the same conclusion—because the child certainly wasn't suffering a common attack of influenza.

'Meningitis?' Alison asked, her eyes deeply worried. At that moment the swing doors opened and Rob McKenzie came hurrying through, his coat tails flapping. He had the slightly embarrassed look of a man who has missed his train, but who hopes to catch it at the next station. 'Good of you to come in, Steve,' he said, coming over to them. 'What do you think?'

'Positive Kernig's sign,' Steve said, and as Rob began to bluster he added quietly, 'If it was negative when you examined her, then we've nipped it in the bud and the prognosis should be good.'

It was easy for Alison to see why the younger man had the senior position. Steve Barrett might look as though he belonged more to the Bondi Beach life-saving team than to a hospital, but there was no denying his ability as a clinician. Alison had seen too many inept examinations and misdiagnoses not to recognise an expert in the field when she saw one. A pity, she decided, watching him carefully, he knew it.

To her chagrin, she was caught in her intense scrutiny, and not for anything did she want him to think he had her interest. 'Lumbar puncture tray, please, Sister,' Steve asked smoothly. 'Oh, and we'd better do a blood culture, throat swab, you know the sort of thing.'

'Yes, of course.' As she started for the treatment room Alison caught sight of student Nurse Molly Slade. The girl's painted little face was scarcely visible under a mass of red hair, on top of which was a barrage of clips anchoring a grubby shred of paper—Alison supposed it was meant to be the regulation cap. Molly was the Medical Superintendent's daughter and since Alison's arrival three weeks back, the girl hadn't lost an opportunity to point it out. Her work was slapdash, her mind on anything but, and Alison had endured about as much as she was going to take of it.

'Nurse Slade,' she said, waylaying the student on her desultory route to the sluice room, 'would you get Emma Fairchild prepared for a lumber puncture, please. You'll find the doctors with her.'

Five minutes later, Alison was back, with a neatly covered trolley containing exactly what would be required. She was annoyed to find Molly perched on Emma's bed, laughing at Steve Barratt's antics.

'Nurse Slade.'

Molly jumped up as if she had been whiplashed, although Alison had spoken her name quietly. She was, as Alison had already discovered, an actress to her fingertips with a career on the stage just waiting for her.

Steve Barratt intervened smoothly, 'We don't think sitting on a bed a crime here, Sister. In fact, if it makes Emma feel happier, Nurse can get into it, as far as I'm concerned.'

Alison smiled, turning calmly to him. 'But nursing discipline isn't your concern, is it, Mr. Barratt.' It was a cool statement of fact.

Steve hesitated for a nicely-judged half-minute; he was going to permit himself the small luxury of putting Sister Prentice in her place, quietly and nicely, of course. And he would have, if some mysterious quality in the luminous greenish eyes hadn't stayed him—and then it was too late, she had turned away.

He watched her move about intent on her work, the chaste line of her uniform not quite concealing the lovely curving line of her back, the nipped-in small waist—she must be younger than twenty-nine, surely—he observed, too, the methodical preparations, the smoothness with which she soon had Molly performing her duties, and her adroitness in circumventing Rob's clumsy procedures that would have contaminated her precious trays.

With everything in readiness and Emma sedated and comfortably positioned in Molly's arms, Steve stepped forward, and by the way Alison snapped on his rubber gloves he knew he had someone who had worked in an operating theatre. His needs were alertly anticipated, it wasn't even necessary to glance up from what he was doing. A good thing too, Steve thought. For he didn't need to be reminded of the eloquence peculiar to her eyes, which were emphasised by the mask she was now wearing. Eyes like that could be an occupational hazard.

After the spinal fluid had been tapped and Emma settled on her back, he stripped his gloves into the discard bag Alison had conveniently taped to the side of the trolley. 'You'll keep an eye on her and see she lies flat for the rest of the day, otherwise she'll have a thumping headache.' But of course it was like preaching to your grandmother. Sister Prentice knew the rules, and had made up a few of her own, he didn't wonder. Probably had a book on nursing procedure already going to print. Anyone with a father like hers was quite equal to it.

'Nurse Slade can sit with Emma until she's awake enough to understand,' Alison said, and directed her next words to Molly. 'You might like to read up on patient after-care while you're at it, Nurse. There's a very good article in the latest *Nursing Journal*. You'll find it in my office.'

'Yes, Sister.'

Steve was still looking at her. Alison could feel his eyes on the back of her neck by the way it prickled. She was suddenly terrified that he might think her incompetent in some way; this job was so important to her. She had come so far, she couldn't make a mess of it now. In her mind she reviewed the procedure they had just completed. Yes, yes, she had done everything, she was sure of it. If she could be sure of anything when he was watching her.

'And clear all that stuff from the top of the locker, please, Nurse. Glass and jug of water only, and please get a cover for it.' She was so nervous her voice had taken on an unpleasant

sharp edge. It was so out of character, Molly hastened to do as
she was asked, without any of her usual arguments. Sister
might be a stickler for discipline, but she was fair, and she
never snapped.

'Oh, come off it, Sister.' Steve caught up with her as she
hurried into the office. 'You're not with a military outfit now.'

Alison refrained from making any remark until she reached
the relative security of her desk. Though even with its solid
reassuring bulk between them she didn't feel quite in control.
It upset her to think someone could shake her confidence in
this way. What was it about him that disturbed her so much?
It couldn't be his physical appearance, she had never been
impressed by men who were too good-looking—they so often
had an ego to match. Her father would have made short work
of him. Taking refuge in this thought, Alison drew herself up
to her full height. It was time he knew who was in charge.

'From the chaotic state of the ward when I took over, Mr
Barratt, I can only assume you are used to a different order of
things. You may equate untidiness and ill discipline with
homeliness. I do not. I intend to run a happy ward, but
procedures will be carried out correctly, if not for the sake of
the students, whose proper training relies on it, then for the
safety of my patients, whose lives do.' Alison stopped short of
breath. She had sounded rather more dramatic than she had
intended, and she hoped she had said nothing ludicrous—long
speeches didn't happen to be her forte.

Steve shuddered. She was serious. A few years back she
would have been out here as a missionary. Now she was going
to make life hell for them, with her zeal for tidiness and
orderliness. Steve raised a laconic brow and muttered, 'No
need to get your knickers in a twist, Sister.' He regretted his
crude remark the moment he heard her indrawn hiss of breath.
He had no need to rub it in. But if she was going to start
prancing around the ward with the rule book, just when he
was trying to get some of them relaxed . . . He stuck his hands
into his pockets and stared belligerently out of the window. He
hoped she wasn't expecting him to apologise, then as the silence
spun out, he thought, oh hell, he'd have to do something to
smooth her down or she would get in a huffy mood and it

would only make things worse.

'I'm sure that basically I agree with what you said.' Whatever that was, he couldn't remember the half of it, she had spoken so quickly. He looked at his watch. 'Now, if there's anything else?'

Alison was still fuming. If he had been a medical student, she would have dismissed him from the ward for making a remark like that. But he wasn't a medical student, he was the Paediatric Registrar—though how anybody who was still only twenty-seven . . . And she had to remind herself that he had given up his free time to come in and see Emma, for which she was very grateful.

'Thank you,' she said, but with little real warmth. 'Emma was our only real worry . . .' She was going to say how thankful she had been that he had turned up, but the words stuck in her throat. In any case he was heading for the door.

'Then I'll see you tomorrow. Ward round at eight sharp.'

'I would prefer nine,' Alison ventured.

A glimmer of a smile showed around Steve's mouth. There was a hint of cruelty there, Alison thought. 'We may be short on formality, but we like an early start in this country. Better get used to it.' The smile widened, and then he was gone.

So that was the brilliant young Registrar everyone raved about. She had so looked forward to meeting him, hoping he would be someone she could talk to—about home, the hospital he had worked at in England, the people he had met. Perhaps they had friends, acquaintances in common. Her throat ached with disappointment when she realised how far short her expectation had fallen in that department. For there would be no eager reminiscing with this young man. Indeed, if they ever got to discuss anything civilly, outside of purely professional matters, it would be nothing short of a miracle.

Later in the afternoon, Alison poured tea into a cup and wondered about Clair Manning, the senior staff nurse she had yet to meet. There were the inevitable rumours linking her with Steve Barratt, and even some speculation as to whether he had gone on holiday with Clair, and bets laid about the possibility of her coming back with an engagement ring on her finger. Alison stared into space, while the tea went cold in the cup. How vividly he came to mind, as if his image had been imprinted there with indelible ink. She grimaced; somehow Alison didn't think Steve Barratt was quite ready to commit himself to anybody, not that young man—but it was high time she got on with her work, instead of sitting around wasting it on thoughts of him.

It was the quietest time of the afternoon and Alison preferred to have tea alone in her office so she could write the report. Mornings, the staff had it together, crammed into a small room off the kitchen. While she was writing, Alison could glimpse through the half-open office door. She knew when the last patient was wheeled back from theatre—although she would be informed in due course by the staff nurse in charge of post-operative patients—she knew when the late afternoon fluids went out, and when the evening paper boy came on his rounds. Well, everyone knew when he came, by his cheery whistle.

Finished her paperwork at last, Alison stood up and stretched. In many ways it had been a satisfying day. Emma was responding to treatment and sleeping peacefully. The croup baby played happily in a moist-air oxygen tent, her breathing difficulties a thing of the past, and nothing too disastrous had happened to the other twenty-six children in her charge. Even the Ivac pumps had been returned, and were now attached to all intravenous lines, so there was no need to worry about any of them going amuck. Of all the luck, having that happen the moment Steve Barratt stepped into the ward! Oh, if only . . . There was no use thinking about it now, she would simply have to do her best to make things go smoothly from now on. But damn the man, he had spoilt everything.

On her way through the hospital corridors to the staff car park, she thought how strange it was that all hospitals had the same smell—that faint mingling of methylated spirits and floor polish overlaid with the aroma of meat pies and boiled cabbage. She knew of people who on leaving the hospital as a place to work had returned years later, seduced back by that very same smell.

Outside, the sun dazzled her eyes. How bright everything

was, and unexpected so late in the afternoon. Even now, the hot colours edging the prim lawns had the power to startle her, as did the palm trees that lined the town streets, with their withered brown leaves rattling in the dry hot wind like so many skeletons. The hospital too had been larger than she imagined; an impressive multi-winged, four-storey concrete building, very modern and slightly out of place with the diminutive wooden houses alongside.

Alison had chosen to live two miles out of the town, in a comfortable old farmhouse which she shared with Anne and Kirstin, both of whom worked at the hospital. The house was rather shabby, but roomy and cosy. Much of their spare time was spent on its wide pillared verandah. There was an acre of land over which eight plump white hens pecked their way during the course of the day. And they had a goat to keep the gorse and hawthorn from overrunning the place. She was beginning to feel very much at home in such an environment, even to the extent of enjoying lying in bed and listening to the sound of rain drumming on the corrugated tin roof.

She turned off the main highway and on to the dusty road leading at first through apple orchards, and then through rolling farmland. But the neat farms seemed to have a precarious hold on the country, for right at their backs were the big sombre bush-covered hills, and beyond, outlined in shades of hazy purple, was the terrible rugged beauty of a tangled range of mountains.

Without any warning, huge drops of rain began to disturb the dust on the windscreen of her little Morris Minor. It always amazed her how the blue untroubled sky could open up in this country, when there wasn't a cloud to be seen. She switched on the wipers and only succeeded in smudging the glass with streaks of brown liquid. Momentarily she was driving blind.

Hastily Alison changed down. But within seconds the torrential rainfall had turned her windscreen into a waterfall. She braked, unable to see the road beyond, and the car skidded out of control.

It happened so quickly, it took several minutes, after lurching into a ditch with a sickening crunch, to work out what had happened, and several more to reach out a shaking hand to turn off the ignition.

Steve Barratt put his Land Rover into low gear and ploughed cautiously along the road, windshield wipers flashing back and forth and only just coping with the downpour. At the bend in the road he saw the small car with its two side wheels in the ditch. He slewed to a stop. From the side compartment he grabbed his first aid case and jumped out.

At first Alison almost failed to recognise him, with his hair plastered to his scalp and rain water dripping from his nose. But his cocky half-amused smile she would know anywhere. She couldn't see why it should comfort her—when he was the last person she wanted to come along and find her stuck so ignominiously in a ditch.

'Like a hand out of there?' Steve asked, his voice provocatively innocent when he saw it was the ice-cool Sister Prentice, and having deduced that she was quite unhurt—or at least from the way she was glaring at him, he supposed she was.

'Thank you,' Alison said stiffly, unsmiling because he was obviously killing himself over having to play the great White Knight to her for the second time in one day. She expected now that he would go on ad nauseam about women drivers.

'I think I must have caught my foot somehow,' Alison muttered through gritted teeth, feeling quite foolish.

'Let's take a gander.' Steve climbed in beside her, filling the small compartment with his wet masculine smell of oilskins and leather and shedding raindrops over her. He reached down and instinctively she tried to draw away, though the hand on her bare legs was surprisingly warm and gentle.

'Sorry, did that hurt?' he asked. 'You've twisted your foot under the pedals. Try and stay still, I'll have you free in a jiff.'

As he wrestled with the foot-piece, Alison didn't know which was worse—her ankle, which was twisted quite painfully, or being half crushed by this bear of a man—and if she detested him so much, she couldn't think why her blood was pounding in her veins in a way it hadn't done for so long.

'There . . . got it. Support yourself on me and wriggle

around a bit,' he commanded. 'You should be able to move your foot once you straighten up.' The soft feel of her hand on his shoulders made him realise how fragile she was, for one who took so much upon herself. 'Right,' he said gruffly, 'that should do it.' He straightened himself up.

'Oh, the relief!' Alison closed her eyes as her foot came free. Her face was very close to his, and Steve found himself studying the pretty curve of her cheek and the way her light brown hair floated down in tendrils. He imagined that it would tumble down in a silky cascade if he were to pull the tight band from her coiled topknot . . . Somewhat bemused, he threw open the door and rather hurriedly clambered on to the road.

'Come on, I'll lift you out.'

'Don't be silly,' she said, embarrassed. 'There's no need, truly. I can manage.' But the car was canted so badly, Alison found she was struggling. I must look like a beached whale, she thought wretchedly. Steve suppressed a grin and reached back in.

'Put your arms around my neck.'

'No, really . . .' she protested feebly. But when he looked at her, as though she were some recalcitrant child confusing her with his mixture of volatile raw energy and easy mollifying charm, she raised her arms and felt his strength set the edge of her senses tingling and the faint ache, only half remembered from another happier time.

The rain felt very welcome and cool on her hot cheeks. Steve let her down and, somewhat gingerly, Alison put her foot to the ground. Still holding her, Steve caught the small spasm of pain that crossed her expression. Without a word he swung her back in his arms and carried her quickly across the road to where the Land Rover waited.

'I'll run you home and take a look at your ankle,' he said, before bundling her into the front seat. Carefully he plucked back a fold of skirt, then shut the door.

'Which way?' he asked, getting in beside her and depositing her car keys and shoulder purse on to her lap.

'The old farmhouse at the fork in the road,' Alison murmured, and he looked at her with lively interest.

'Well, well, so you've moved in with Anne and Kirstin,' as if in some way she had risen higher in his esteem. 'I live a few miles farther on.'

'Oh . . .' Alison digested this news as his hand on the gear shift brushed against her thigh. Her eyes dropped. There was something very reassuring about a man's clean capable hand. She studied his watch—quiet, solid, absolutely reliable, and she knew, very expensive—and the way the short blond hairs lay on his wrist. A few minutes later she was home.

When they came to a standstill outside the front gate, Steve jumped out. Alison hopped down without waiting for his assistance. 'Thank you,' she said, when he came round the bonnet. 'I don't know what I'd have done if you hadn't come along when you did.'

He looked at her standing on one foot, a hand gripping the door handle. 'Better let me help you in, I think.' Alison was insisting on trying it herself, when Kristin came drifting down the path.

'Hello . . . My hat, what happened? Alison, are you all right?'

'Yes, yes, fine,' Alison said cheerfully, hoping that Steve Barratt might take himself off in his Land Rover now that he had seen her safely home. He had been very kind, and she wasn't ungrateful, though she wished fervently it had been anybody but him. It was enough that she was in his debt now—a state of affairs she imagined he wouldn't be slow to capitalise on.

'Take her other arm,' Steve said, completely ignoring Alison and addressing himself to Kirstin with one of his impossibly charming smiles. While they went slowly up the path he explained what had happened. At the verandah steps, he simply picked her up as if she were a featherweight, letting Kirstin lead the way into their comfortable if untidy front room. Once the couch had been cleared of its occupants—two disgruntled tabbies and a disdainful Siamese—Alison was lowered on to the cushions. Kirstin hovered by making little noises of sympathy and then went on a search for elastic bandages.

Alison's foot and ankle were by now badly swollen and painful, so that when Steve began his careful examination, she had to bite back an exlamation. 'You did twist it badly,' he murmured. 'Sorry, I'll be as gentle as I can.' Alison dropped her head back on a cushion, listening to the reassuring murmur of his voice while his fingers probed gently at muscles and tendons.

'Found some in the bathroom cabinet,' Kirstin said, returning with the bandages Steve required. She kneeled down by his side and began tearing off the cellophane. She was a fully trained physiotherapist and an expert at strapping injured parts, and she teased Steve on his technique, to which he responded with a ready banter. The two were engrossed in what they were doing, Kirstin's head of cropped blonde curls close to Steve's. They seemed so at ease with each other, so perfectly in tune, Alison began to feel an outsider. Her sense of exclusion increased as she watched them.

But what man wouldn't find Kirstin irresistible? Alison thought. Like Steve, she was a golden girl, her fresh Nordic beauty inherited from Scandinavian parents, a perfect skin that tanned to a shade of liquid honey and didn't burn and freckle, as Alison's did . . .

'How does that feel?' Steve asked, and she coloured when she realised his eyes were upon her.

'Oh—yes . . . It feels good, thank you.' She smiled, but it seemed tight, meaningless, too polite. Kirstin meanwhile had jumped up with her bubbling laugh and was offering to make tea.

'Wonderful. I'll come and help,' Steve said. Did she imagine relief in his voice? He followed Kirstin, but at the door he turned with a reminder. 'Remember, keep that leg up.' It was incredible how foolish Alison felt, with her leg in the air and people having to do things for her. A few minutes later, she heard Anne's car pull up outside.

'Ye god's!' Anne said, after Alison had explained. 'When I saw your car in the ditch . . .' She inspected Steve's work with a Theatre Sister's critical eyes, then said, 'Where's Steve now?'

'Kitchen, helping make tea,' Alison gave a little laugh. 'He seems right at home here.'

'Oh, he used to be a regular visitor before Clair entered his life. Still drops in occasionally, though of course he's been on on holiday since you've been here.'

'Who's taking my name in vain?' Steve demanded, arriving with a full tray. On it, beside the tea things, were a glass of water and a bottle of tablets. 'Take two and repeat four-hourly for pain if needed,' he ordered Alison, who hesitated, her face betraying her uncertainty when he offered her two in a teaspoon. A smile gleamed in his eyes.

'See,' he said, appealing to the other two. 'She doesn't trust me.' And then he had turned back to her and his tone was serious again. 'It's only a codeine-based painkiller I carry in my bag.' Alison still hesitated. She had a deep aversion to taking drugs of any kind, unless it was absolutely necessary. But for people who handled them every day it was only too easy, and pain was often the first excuse to start.

'No need to suffer when you don't have to.' Steve Barratt's voice held a note of derision. Oh, it was carefully concealed in the light bantering tone, but Alison realised it; she also realised that he didn't like her one little bit. Well, she thought coldly, the feeling was mutual.

'Thank you, Doctor,' she said, forcing a light tone and taking the tablets if only to keep the other two from guessing at the animosity that lay like a slit-eyed monster between them. And from now on, that was the way it would have to be. She must act cordially towards him, if only for the sake of the children under their care.

Alison sat sipping her tea while Steve chatted amicably with Anne and Kirstin. Her thoughts were far away when he rose to go. 'You'd better take the next few days off,' he said, looking down at her.

'I couldn't possibly,' Alison objected. 'The ward is so busy.' Remembering to be pleasant to him, she smiled brightly. 'Oh, don't worry, the swelling will be down by tomorrow morning. I'll be fine.'

'You don't have to be a hero. Clair will be back tomorrow and she can take over,' Steve replied smoothly, and she saw that Clair taking over would suit him just fine. Of course then, with Sister out of the way, life would be easy again. Routine would be lax, nobody would worry too much about discipline and if the students learnt nothing, and the dressings didn't get changed as often as they should, so what.

Her voice was crabbed, despite every effort to the contrary. 'I'll see how I'm feeling tomorrow,' she smiled up at him in a grim effort. 'Thank you for everything.'

The woman went out of her way to be difficult, thought Steve, shuddering at the prospect of having her come in to limp about the place, making life miserable for herself as well as everyone else. 'I'll see that Burt tows your car along to his garage,' he told her, before turning to blow a kiss at Anne and Kirstin. 'Thanks for the tea, girls.'

'Why did he have to go and fall for someone like Clair?' Anne said, when he had gone. 'You watch out for that girl,' she warned Alison, 'she's a real little madam.'

Kirstin stirred dreamily. 'Gorgeous, isn't he? You couldn't possibly not like him, Alison.'

Alison agreed. Oh, he was gorgeous. But like him she certainly did not.

CHAPTER TWO

THE REPORT lay open in front of her. Alison frowned with impatience after a brief glance at her watch and tapped the desk with the tip of her pencil. 'We can't wait a moment longer. I'll begin with the side rooms.' The nurses ringed round her desk fell into a respectful silence.

'Peter McBride,' Alison started crisply, 'eleven-year-old boy who was admitted two days ago with acute appendicitis and taken straight to theatre . . .' Her voice faded as the door opened, and ten pairs of eyes swivelled with undisguised interest to witness Clair Manning's late arrival.

'Sorry . . .' The slender, dark-haired girl who entered the room was all smiling apology, her tawny eyes settling on Alison as she introduced herself, then passing on to acknowledge the murmured greetings of the others.

Alison waited until Clair had made her elegant way to a chair, before pushing on with the report. The minutes were running by and she had to be finished by eight, the staff allocated their jobs — never mind see that all the children were on their right beds. Eight sharp, Steve had said, in that domineering voice she had begun to hate.

By dint of rattling along and giving out orders in the kind of astringent voice the assembled nurses thought best not argue with, Alison managed to finish on time. Though it wasn't how she liked to do things. She much preferred to take longer over the report, stopping to discuss the important issues and each child in detail, and to make sure everyone knew exactly what was expected of them. The schedule, however, was not of her making. Doctors did their rounds when it suited them, and had to be worked around, unless of course they could be reasoned with. Fat chance she had with a man like Steve Barratt. Alison sighed and stood up.

'Well, that's it for now. Staff Manning, if you could make sure the twins at the end haven't swopped beds again. I'm sure you remember them from before you went on holiday,' adding in a light touch of humour, 'Impossible to forget them, I expect. Anyway, Mr Barratt will want the children to be on their own beds.'

'Oh, don't worry, Sister . . .' Clair's tone told Alison how very boring it was of her to fuss. 'Steve never minds, so long as all the kids can be accounted for, somewhere along the line.'

'But I do worry, Staff.' And her level gaze made it clear just how much. 'And please, on duty could we use surnames.' Alison closed the subject by turning to the Kardex trolley, the straightness of her back the only indication of her annoyance with the senior staff nurse's attitude.

Quickly she got the folders into the order they would be needed on the round, checking as she went—treatment charts, laboratory forms, prescription pads. Satisfied she had everything, she released the footbrake and struggled to pull the cumbersome trolley to the door.

'Well, good morning, Alison. I see your injury hasn't kept you away from work.' Steve Barratt lounged against the office door in a doctor's coat of impeccable whiteness. Underneath, she observed a white open-necked shirt and walking shorts, also very clean and pressed, and she caught the gleam of highly polished shoes. He at least had taken some trouble with his appearance, she was forced to admit, and noticing with irrational interest the knee-high elegance of his white cable-stitched socks.

'Here, let me.' With his infuriating grin he gave the brake lever a swift kick and twirled the trolley easily into its place in the corridor. Looking down at her, he said with deadpan seriousness, 'You've just got to show the thing who's boss, Alison.'

'Thank you Mr Barratt,' she murmured, still somewhat bemused by his appearance, 'but I think I'll get the engineers to have a look at it. Save me wearing out my shoes.' She watched as he began to rifle through her neat piles of folders. 'And please,' she implored, 'I've only just got those arranged in order of beds.' She turned as Rob and Stuart came through the wing doors, their ties and long trousers eliciting an amused look from Clair, who had sauntered up to join them. Alison was begining to regret Stuart's uninvited gesture to make her feel more at home, heartwarming though it had been at the time. She had hardly expected Rob to follow his example, though.

'Sure you can manage on that foot?' Steve asked, after greetings had been exchanged.

'Yes, fine, thank you,' Alison replied sharply, thinking how effective his lazy smiles were at hiding what he was really about. They moved off, Alison walking stiffly by Steve Barratt's side, determined not to show any sign of a limp, though her ankle bothered her more than a little. Rob and Clair followed and Stuart was left to bring up the rear with the cranky trolley. Obviously he hadn't been given the benefit of Steve Barratt's advice, Alison thought with a certain malicious satisfaction, for the young doctor was having as much trouble getting it to run smoothly as she had.

'What have we here, Sister?'

Steve Barratt's cold voice sliced into her thoughts. They had entered Peter McBride's room and Alison's startled gaze fell on a child who was sweaty and pale and in obvious distress. 'Peter McBride . . . second day post-op,' she managed before he again cut in.

'I know that. I did his operation.' There was nothing relaxed about the man now. But Alison was too preoccupied to notice, for something was terribly wrong.

'Peter, you haven't eaten anything, have you?' she queried anxiously as the child groaned. Whereupon Clair held up a half-eaten bunch of grapes. Alison felt like groaning herself, for the child was restricted to fluids only, following an operation where handling of the intestines caused them to become temporarily paralysed. With food in his stomach there was a very real danger of obstruction.

'Better let me take a look at that tum of yours.' Steve settled himself on the bed and in his deceptively lazy way began to examine Peter's abdomen. 'Distended all right,' he muttered, spearing Alison with a savage glance, as if she'd force-fed the unfortunate boy his grapes.

'We'll see if we can't get rid of that stuff for you, Peter, eh?' he said gently. Peter's nod was doubtful, but apparently anything was better than the pain in his stomach. Steve said curtly to Alison, 'Ryles number eight should do it.'

When she returned with a trolley and everything necessary to put down a nasal gastric tube, Steve wandered over. 'Hope this will do the trick,' he muttered, adding sarcastically, 'There may be anything down there, meat pies, who knows?'

'Well, Mr Barratt, we shall soon find out,' Alison replied, outwardly calm when in fact he was making her as nervous as a kitten. She hoped he would go on his round and leave her to it. But Steve was quite happy to stay and watch.

Of course, there wasn't one thing he could fault her on. She had the Ryles tube up and over in a flawless display of technique, before Peter was even aware of it. He noted, too, that she was in the stomach and not in the lungs—which was as easy to do as it was embarrassing.

'It's gastric juice,' Alison murmured, watching the litmus turn colour. As well, she thought, because she couldn't stand to give him the satisfaction of blundering under his very nose. It was bad enough knowing they had slipped up somewhere, though she couldn't see how. Peter's visitors knew not to leave food. Even so, there was a routine inspection after visiting hours, because inevitably, some well-meaning person would leave a bag of food, feeling sorry for a child, and especially one who claims to be starving, not knowing the danger a paralytic ileus could cause.

'Good,' Steve growled. She was beginning to fascinate him. Did nothing daunt her? he wondered, watching Alison withdraw a quantity of partially digested food from Peter's stomach without so much as turning a hair. He had to hand it to her, she was good at her job, and lucky for him she was, but he shuddered. Save him from women like that!

Clair meanwhile had found something more congenial to watch from the window, and it did cross Steve's mind that she could be more helpful. But it was a notion he dismissed instantly. Sister would probably consider any help to be an interference, and in any case, Clair was sensitive, easily upset by the more gruesome side of nursing, try as she might to hide it.

The next patient was Kiri Mata, the tot with croup who had come in the day before. 'Still on two-hourly inhalations, Sister?' Steve bent over and pretended to examine Kiri's teddy, much to the child's glee. 'Any sign of laryngeal obstruction through the night?' he asked, straightening up, and knowing Alison would have the answer for him without having to refer to the night report. Kiri meanwhile had proffered up her teddy and Clair was obliged to execute a neat sidestep out of the way. The thing looked positively revolting, and ridden with infection, she shouldn't wonder. In her opinion the wretched toy ought to be consigned to the hospital furnace.

Steve was discussing Kiri's treatment with Stuart and Alison, and it was Rob who took it from the child's hand. 'Have we got anything for alopecia, Doctor?' he asked in mock seriousness, referring to the balding areas on the poor bear.

'Sister's bound to think of something that will help,' Steve said, looking up from a chart. He went over and firmly placed Teddy back in Kiri's arms. The child looked at him adoringly. It was easy to see why children loved him, and women. She wouldn't be a bit surprised if he hadn't left a trail of broken hearts, Alison thought drily to herself, watching Clair follow his every movement with her eyes.

Were the rumours true? she wondered. Was he having a love affair with her? There was no outward evidence to support the theory. Not that it interested her one way or the other. She had conveniently forgotten that her own eyes too had fallen with unerring accuracy on Clair's slim, white, but ringless finger that morning.

Out in the corridor again, Steve said, 'I'll pop along and have a look at young Emma Fairchild.' Or was that going to upset the order of her precious folders? he wondered, noticing the look of strain on Alison's pale face. Perhaps it was that injured foot of hers she insisted on stalking about the place on when she should be resting it up on a couch—preferably the one back at her own house. He saw that she still had the strapping on.

'Of course,' Alison said stiffly, having noted the steely look from the otherwise sleepy blue eyes. It was a bit like finding a needle in a haystack, that look of his, she thought, irritated because her leg was bothering her more and more and she dared not let on about it now. This morning when she got up, it had felt fine.

'What have we got here, Nurse?' Alison asked Hine Te Atawhai, a sunny-natured Maori girl who was peering doubtfully into a pan of orange puree.

'Don't know, Sister. Don't know whether it's mashed up veg, or if it's pud. The label's come off.'

'Looks like pureed carrots to me,' Alison said, looking puzzled herself when she found the dish was cold. 'Get a spoon and have a taste, Hine, and if you're still not sure we'll send it back.' While the student hurried towards the kitchen, presumably to get a spoon, which ought to have been on the trolley anyway, Alison went ahead with serving out.

The morning hours had fled past with their usual unnerving speed, despite the trouble her leg was causing her, and the chaotic round where Steve Barratt had chosen to chop and change instead of going through the ward systematically — as if to deliberately upset her, though it was the wasted time Alison resented more than anything. The report on the doctor's round had taken longer than usual. This was given during morning tea: a veritable feast of a meal that surprised Alison daily with its abundance of buttered bread and accompanying spreads, scones and toasted cheese sandwiches, and because one of the students had a birthday, that morning there was a large cake with candles as well. Then it was the arranged admissions to sort out, and anxious parents to reassure. More often than not the children, those who were well enough, headed without so much as a backward glance for the exciting-looking play area outside the open doors. But the ward had settled down in time to see the first lot of nurses to their own lunch, and now Alison was serving up the children's meal.

'Light diets first,' she said cheerfully to Jenny Duncan who had come hurrying up with a pile of trays. 'These can be for the twins . . .' She paused as a buzzer went and turned to look down the ward. 'It's Billy,' she said, shoving back a tray of food into the hot compartment. 'He's the new bronchial asthma patient Molly's admitting . . .'

'He can't breathe,' Molly whispered, her eyes blinking with fright. Though Alison quickly ascertained that Molly's claim wasn't strictly correct, she didn't blame her in the least for thinking so, for Billy's laboured breathing was so prolonged in expiration, it was enough to frighten the wits out of anybody, let alone a junior nurse. His cyanosed state, wheezing and profuse sweating signified a severe asthma attack, and Alison, using extreme caution, knowing well the risks inherent in giving an asthmatic child oxygen, set about administering it without further waste of time.

'Better get Mr. Barratt,' she told Jenny in a low voice. 'If Billy doesn't respond to the nebuliser, we may have to give him the drug intravenously.' Jenny needed no prompting—one look at the child's thin shoulders hunched in a pitiful attempt to get air in and out of his lungs sent her flying in the direction of the office phone.

To comfort the distraught child, Alison took him on her lap, encouraging him gently to take the nebulised drug via a face mask. In a remarkably short time his breathing was less laboured and Alison was able to smile up at an anxious Molly, who was still hovering by her side. 'I think we're winning. If you don't mind going now and helping with the rest of the lunches, I can manage here.' By the time Steve arrived, Billy was curled up, cradled in Alison's arms, almost asleep. Despite himself, Steve was strangely moved by the sight.

'It was a severe attack, he was cyanosed,' Alison said, immediately taking up a defensive position when she saw his eyes on the oxygen equipment and knowing what was on his mind.

Steve Barratt nodded, for it was obvious to him that Alison's quick intervention had done the trick. Severe attacks could develop into status asthmaticus in a quite terrifyingly short space of time. 'You did very well,' he said thoughtfully, his eyes on the child in her arms. 'Though we may still have to put up a drip, in which case I'd like an experienced nurse to special him in a side room for the next few days while we run some tests.'

'Staff Nurse Manning will be back from lunch very soon.' Even as Alison spoke, Clair appeared in the ward. She might just as well have come straight from the beauty salon. Every hair of the swinging bob was in place, sparkling white cap just so, lips carefully outlined and filled in with a paler colour to give that natural look. Well, Alison thought wryly, she couldn't fault Clair's attention to her appearance; she looked the perfect senior staff nurse, cool, alert, supremely professional. And Alison at that moment felt hot, sticky and untidy, with her hair coming down in wisps and her left foot and ankle, ugly in its bulky strapping, undeniably painful.

'Oh,' Clair digested the news with considerable distaste. She much preferred being in the ward, ushering doctors around and dispensing orders to the junior nurses, to being stuck in a side room. But Steve was watching her and he had been acting very oddly all morning. She might have wondered if perhaps he wasn't interested in the new Sister, though she dismissed that as unlikely. Alison, with her mousy hair, wasn't the sort of woman Steve went for, and she was hardly the type to want to entice him away. Besides, she was older than Steve. And to twenty-year-old Clair, twenty-nine seemed—well, middle-aged. Over the hill anyway. No, it wasn't Alison she had to worry about, it was Kirstin Peterson. Suppressing a sigh, she said, 'Oh well, of course.'

'Great—so that's settled.' Steve gave Billy an encouraging pat on the arm. 'You just keep puffing away there, sonny, and we'll have you right as rain in no time.' Then as Clair headed off to supervise the change-over, he turned to Alison with a half smile.

'Don't forget Matron's farewell in the library.'

Alison had forgotten. What was more to the point, she didn't have time now. Already she was aware of slipping behind her schedule, and a distinct panicky feeling she was never going to catch up—though she had a chance if she worked on through her lunch hour. Good heavens, there was a pile of work on her desk that would keep her busy for a week—the kitchen stores orders the ward maid wanted her to sign, the laundry lists . . . She managed a careless little laugh.

'Think perhaps I'll take it easy, have a quiet bite to eat in my office and put my foot up.'

'How is it holding out?' Steve queried politely.

'Fine, fine . . .'

'Good, then why don't you come along and join us. Kill two birds with one stone. Have lunch and meet the new Matron at the same time.' He grinned. 'In fact, you can't afford not to come and hear what she has to say. Forewarned is forearmed, so they say.'

'What do you mean by that?' Alison asked sharply, perturbed by the cheesy grin and not trusting him for a second.

'Come and find out,' he suggested, with another wide grin, then he turned and sauntered down the ward, hands thrust into his shorts pockets, his white coat bunched untidily behind him. She stared after him, noting that his hair was far too long at the back, and trying to work out why shorts and knee-high socks didn't look incongruous under a doctor's coat when to her mind, that combination should. But it didn't, not even slightly.

'You can't go mixing politics with sport . . .' Stuart was holding forth about his favourite pastime, rugby. Anne was amongst the group; she detached herself when Alison arrived and hurried over.

'Goodness, I was thinking you were never going to get here. As it is, you've missed the speeches and most of the food has gone. Some sandwiches left, though, I kept you a plate, and there's plenty of wine.' She studied Alison with a frown. 'You look all in, I'll go and grab you a glass of the old pick-me-up.' Alison caught hold of her arm before she could disappear into the crowd—it appeared that the entire hospital had turned out to see Matron Brown off and welcome Jean Pettit, the new one.

'Did you hear what Jean Pettit had to say?'

'Got here just in time. Pity you missed it. It's your department she's intent on turning upside down. Bit of a cheek, I thought, old Browny not even out of the door and she's airing her new ideas. Talk about a new broom sweeping clean. We knew it was coming, of course.'

'I didn't know it was coming,' Alison said, thoroughly alarmed now. 'Nobody said anything to me.'

'You must have heard that the nursing staff in the children's ward will go into mufti. Steve Barratt's always on about it. He'd like to see the nurses in jeans and trainers, and he wants the visiting hours altered so relatives can visit when they want. He couldn't do anything with Browny, but apparently he has Jean Pettit eating out of his hand. Look, I'll get you those sandwiches, won't be a tick.' Alison watched her go. So that was the reason Steve had been so pleased with himself. She was the Sister, and he hadn't even bothered to tell her himself. Alison was angry—but aware also of a transitory pain that he had treated her so casually.

She was startled from her pensive thoughts when Stuart loomed up by her side bearing a tray with several glasses of wine and a plate heaped with things to eat, the variety of which suggested little discrimination in their choosing. 'Bit of a scrum there for a while. Didn't see you around, so I grabbed something to put aside in case you missed out. Got to be early for this kind of do.'

Stuart had the look of a man who had fought a long hard battle, but who had finally succeeded in dragging home the fatted calf. Alison had a wild desire to giggle. What on earth was she going to do with it all? And he couldn't possibly expect her to consume several glasses of wine. And then Anne was back.

'Sorry, old thing. Got to go and set up for a case.' She deposited a plate of sandwiches in Alison's hands. 'Hello, Stuart, not still eating? Your boss is looking for you.' She darted away, only to rush back again. 'I can give you a lift home if you want it, Alison—that's if we get finished in time. Cherry.'

'Lord . . .' Stuart muttered, 'I'm supposed to be over at the nurses' tutorial. I told Steve I'd stand in for him. Here, you take these, I'd better be off.' And Alison was left standing with a tray of food and wine in one hand and a plate of sandwiches in the other.

'My, my, my, and you said you only wanted a bite to eat.'

Steve Barratt had a grin from ear to ear. 'And was that young Stuart I saw you with? Didn't he mention anything about a nurses' tutorial before he rushed away?'

'He did, and if you saw him with me you'd know that he left me with all this food.' Steve laughed, and took the tray from her, handing her back a fork wrapped in a napkin.

'What say I hold on to it and we'll both share, the sandwiches can go on here as well. I must confess to having missed out as well.' He reached for the plate she was holding. His hands were large and steady, unfussy, reassuring hands, and for a second one of them completely covered her own, as he took the plate. Quickly she released her hold on it and drew away. Had he done it deliberately? Her heart lurched in her chest and she stared at the glass of wine he was now offering her.

'Oh . . . Thank you.' Alison took a large gulp and nearly choked. For a moment they were silent, Steve munching hungrily through a chicken leg and Alison nibbling at some kind of savoury pastry. It tasted vaguely like oysters, a delicacy she wasn't very fond of, but which was relished with gusto by every true-blue New Zealander. The wretched thing seemed to swell in her mouth. She took another large gulp of wine, managing to swallow it over.

'So,' she said, hanging on to the remains of the pastry and hoping he wouldn't notice she wasn't eating, 'did you miss the new Matron's speech as well?'

''fraid so. These things are good.' Alison watched as one pastry after the other disappeared into his mouth. 'But I happen to know what it was all about.' He smiled engagingly at her. 'Want me to tell you?'

How smug he was. 'Not particularly,' Alison replied. 'Anne has pretty well filled me in. I take it you want the staff in jeans and trainers.'

'If that's what they feel most comfortable in—why not?' Steve looked down at her with his most benign smile, and Alison tensed herself, already knowing that smile to be his most dangerous. 'Ah, but you don't approve, do you, I can see it written all over your face. Well,' he drawled, 'I didn't expect that any daughter of Sir Charles Prentice would.' Steve picked up another drumstick and his strong white teeth flashed in a smile.

'You know that I was his Junior Registrar,' he said, hugely enjoying the look of frozen surprise on her face. Anyone so far from home might be expected to be thrilled to find some person who had been in such close contact with her father. Not Alison, apparently—he proceeded cheerfully to demolish the chicken in a few bites, laying the bone down on the plate with a surgeon's neat precision, and tempting fate with a further remark.

'If your old man came across someone on his ward wearing jeans, he'd have apoplexy, I swear.'

'I don't think that's funny,' Alison snapped, and Steve was taken aback by the anger blazing in her eyes. He'd only been having a joke with her.

'I'm sorry, Alison, please don't take me too seriously, I'm only a rough Colonial, after all.' His voice held a note of facetiousness, but when he saw she wasn't amused, he quickly adopted a more respectful air. 'How is your father, anyway?' He wanted to win her over to his side on the forthcoming issues, so he didn't wish to upset her unnecessarily.

Alison bit her lip, too proud to show any emotion, too angry and indignant to answer. But then, she thought, after all he couldn't know. He wouldn't be that cruel. Steve found himself waiting tensely for her to reply, staring at the secretive mouth, the equally sensuous droop at each corner, and wondering if anybody had kissed those lips as they ought to have been kissed. And then the luminous eyes settled on his face.

'My father died six months ago,' she said flatly. 'Of a stroke, or as you put is so nicely, Mr. Barratt, apoplexy. Though not, I assure you, from anything so trivial as you suggest. My father wasn't like that. He was never bothered by trivial things.'

Steve's eyes closed involuntarily, and he groaned inwardly. Of all the bloody fool things to have said! He looked at her, and she looked steadily back at him. If there had been an outcry, a storm, a protest, he could have handled it better. 'Look,' he stammered, 'I'm terribly sorry, I had no idea.' He grimaced. 'You see, I lost touch after I left England. And you're right, your father wasn't bothered by trivia. He had a very fine mind and it was always on problems relating to ways he could best help the children under his care. I had no right to say what I did.'

'Well,' and there was the faintest glimmer of a smile lurking around her eyes, 'he wasn't the easiest of men . . .' It was an admission of a sort, and Steve understood in a flash that it was also a very small concession to him. But that was all there ever could be, for she wasn't disposed towards being disloyal. He saw that, and admired her for it.

'He would be very proud of you,' Steve said, his voice husky with the realisation that through this minor act of understanding between them they had somehow broken through a barrier.

'I hope so,' Alison said, before she quite had her voice under control. Oh yes, she hoped so, and yet so often she felt she had been a disappointment to him—quiet and hard-working, intelligent, but never brilliant, never the son he had wanted. A son to follow after him, the old school, and then Cambridge, one of the good medical schools. A son he could talk to. It wasn't possible to talk to a woman, he had said it often.

And then he'd never really got over the shame of having his only daughter left standing at the altar on her wedding day—though in reality she had never stepped from the car, but it amounted to the same thing. Alison suspected he had blamed her more, because for her father, the sun rose and shone on Dr. James Albert Houghton. He simply wasn't able to believe that the man whose reputation as the brightest young houseman of the year was known to one and all could jilt his daughter without good reason.

And Alison, in desperation, had offered him one, indeed, she had almost got round to believing it herself. But looking back, she knew now that James had never been ready to make a real commitment. He had simply evaded the issue, as he had evaded so many in his young life, having wealth and good looks and a family who always settled up for him. On the day he was to be married, he had been out cold on his bed after a night-long drinking session—something that happened far too frequently, and which naturally Alison had kept from her father in the stupid belief that it would be different after they were married. But from that day—a legacy from that frightful hour-long wait driving round and around the block until she was sick with nerves—from that day, she resolved, never would she again trust a man with her life and happiness.

'Alison . . .?' Her face had the closed withdrawn look of a person remembering something too painful to talk about. Steve said softly, 'Look, why don't we . . .' He was going to suggest they talk some time about it, thinking it might help to unburden herself to a sympathetic person—it wasn't much fun being a stranger and so far from home, as well he remembered—but she cut in with a startled exclamation.

'Oh God, is that the time? I don't know what I can be thinking about. I must get back to the ward, I've simply oodles of paperwork to do.' She edged her nibbled pastry back on to the tray with a quick, half embarrassed smile, as if she had only just discovered it in her hand and couldn't imagine how it got there. 'See you later.' Before he knew it, she had turned and was making her way through the straggling groups towards the door.

'Wait a moment . . .' Steve dumped the tray on a convenient chair and dashed after her, causing a few heads to turn in interest.

'Alison,' he said, coming up behind her and falling into step. 'Look, I've got an appendix in theatre to do, they're setting up for it now. I was wondering, why don't you come down and assist me?' He allowed his question to hang there for a moment, then followed it up by saying encouragingly, 'I could tell you'd worked in theatre, by the way you assisted with that lumbar puncture. And it'd beat doing paperwork. Wouldn't you agree?'

'Yes, I'll say.' She was tempted. Then she shrugged. 'It's got to be done all the same.'

'You worry too much,' Steve assured her. 'Clair used to shove it in the top drawer and nothing bad ever happened to her. Anyway, it's my theory that paper work makes for more paperwork and so on. And so therefore . . .' That was just the kind of irresponsible stand he would take, and it was precisely because Clair had stuck it away out of sight in the first place that she had so much to do now. She stopped short, beside him, an odd inscrutability shuttering her gaze.

'And therefore,' she continued for him, 'if I just ignore it, the problem will fade away.' It was the way James would have reasoned. And it occurred to her, not for the first time, how very like him Steve Barratt was.

Steve frowned, it wasn't quite what he'd been going to say, but he let it go. 'Well, whatever,' he said easily, adding with a quick grin, 'But if you go round there now, you won't get much done. Jean Pettit is hoping to see you unofficially and I know for a fact she has the next two hours at her disposal to discuss the changes she's planning.'

A full-scale meeting was not what Alison felt like—not just yet. She much preferred finding out first what exactly was proposed so that she could have her own thoughts clear when she met the Matron. The way she was feeling at the moment, she could be bulldozed into agreeing to anything. She had the weekend off, and she would think about it then.

'But I can hardly avoid her,' she murmured, a mute appeal in her voice that Steve was quick to note. He hid a smile.

'Yes, you can. I'll get Sister McCully to ring through and say you're in theatre. That should go down well, because apparently our new Matron approves of her Sisters keeping their hand in with all spheres of nursing. She also says it shows a person has confidence in her staff when they can delegate responsibility and leave the ward for an hour or two.'

'Does it?' murmured Alison, thinking that Steve Barratt knew a great deal about what had been said, for one who claimed to have missed hearing it in the first place. But of course, she had forgotten, he had Jean Pettit eating out of his hand.

However, she had made her mind up. For one thing, she enjoyed theatre work, for another, being present during surgery was always a valuable reminder—sometimes too easily forgotten—of the trauma a patient underwent in the process of any normal operation. As if on cue, the lift doors slid silently open a few feet from where she stood. For an instant, Alison felt his hand warm on the small of her back as she allowed him to guide her in.

A few minutes later she was accompanying him along the

ground floor corridor to the large swing doors at the end marked, 'Operating Theatre Personnel Only.' Once inside, the corridors were hushed by acoustic ceilings, their walls shining cleanly with a light warm pastel paint. In the background came the familiar hum of the closed air circulating system.

'This is your changing room.' Steve opened the door and ushered her in. 'You'll find everything you need. Change and go on through the door at the end—I'll meet you there.'

The routine was known to Alison, as was the layout of the room she found herself in—the shower unit and toilet facilities and the long row of lockers, and at the other end, across a dividing bench, the rows of individual clogs owned by the girls who wore them in theatre. Alison paused, looking for the light cotton dresses that were worn under the sterile gowns, and which were normally to be found amongst the piles of caps and paper over-shoes. There were none on the shelves, or anywhere else for that matter. Perplexed, she continued her search. Nothing. At last she noticed a side door leading off from the shower unit. She threw it open, expecting to find a linen room. Instead it was the men's changing room, and she had blundered in on Steve Barratt, who was stripping his shirt to reveal a broad strong back, smooth and brown as an egg.

'Not lost, by any chance?' His mouth twitched as he turned and saw her standing in the doorway like a startled deer, and for once, looking anything but in control of herself.

'I . . . No—I mean, I'm looking for something to put on,' Alison blurted, more embarrassed than she had ever been in her entire life. And why she just stood there, and hadn't immediately withdrawn, was something she didn't care to contemplate.

'The linen trolley gets left out back on the odd occasion, if the girls are too busy to unpack it. Sorry, I should have checked for you.' He casually pulled on a green short-sleeved vest. 'I'll just change my strides and hunt something up.' Quite deliberately he began unbuckling his belt, chuckling to himself as Alison spun about and snapped the door shut behind her.

With her cheeks flaming, Alison slumped down on the wooden dividing bench and propped her leg up, only half aware of how badly it ached. Damn the man! She might have been referring to his teasing action, designed to bait her primness, she knew, but was as much again attributed to her own irrational desire at the time, to reach out and touch that warm brown back.

Her head was down, the palms of her hands sliding gingerly up over her bandaged ankle, when Steve appeared with a pile of cotton dresses. In his enthusiasm, he had forgotten her injury, and now he looked at her with concern, noticing the tight look of pain around her eyes.

Quickly she placed her foot to the floor. 'Thank you,' she said, not looking at him. 'Just put them down there, I'll be ready in a moment.'

'You sure?' He was watching her, his blue eyes intent. 'Foot not bothering you too much?' Alison shook her head vigorously—much too vigorously, and he added, 'Look, let's forget it this time. McCully's got more staff than she knows what to do with today.' He could tell by her doubtful look she didn't believe it, any more than he did himself. The eyes under the straight brows regarded him steadily. Did she never get out in the sun? he wondered, suddenly exasperated by the milky opaqueness of her skin, as much as with the shadowed unhappiness in the wide eyes. Then, for some reason lost to him, he bent and dropped a light kiss on her forehead. Her skin was satiny, deliciously cool on his lips.

Alison stopped breathing. And then the realisation hit her. How dare he! She wasn't some young nurse fresh from Prelim school. Oh, she was quite aware of what her reaction should be—it was just that her body seemed to have been reprogrammed.

It had been an impulse, nothing more, and Steve meant to laugh it off with a joking remark. That was what he meant to do—not succumb to the trembling softness of her mouth like some hot-headed youth. He felt her quiver, as desire darkened her senses like a powerful wine with its sweet promise until she was gasping and helpless and her mouth was slackening, opening to his. And then she had jerked away from him and was on her feet quickly, her face flaming, denying what had happened and willing him to do the same with an accusing flickering glance.

'You'd better go along to the Physio department and get some treatment for that foot of yours,' he said gruffly, feeling a perfect fool. God, the last thing he wanted was for the woman to think he had any designs on her. What on earth had got into him?

He had been trying her out—that much was obvious. Less so, was the wild beating of her heart, if she had but stopped to think. 'There's no need,' Alison snapped, seeking refuge in anger. 'I'm all right . . .'

'The hell you are,' Steve snarled softly, standing over her. 'You've been limping round all day with that pained expression on your face.' Pained expression? What pained expression? Now she was really mad. For the first time in her life, Alison came close to shouting at a colleague. Seething, she drew herself up to her full height, wishing she had an extra six or seven inches so she could look him straight in the eye, instead of always having to put up with the patronising way he had of looking down his arrogant nose at her. She hadn't realised before now just how arrogant it was.

Steve's voice had sunk to a dangerously low level. 'Go home and be a martyr if you want, but at the hospital, so long as I'm around, you'll have treatment whether you like it or not, and if you can't get there on your own two feet, I'll carry you. Failing that, I'll call a porter and have you wheeled . . .' Whatever else he might have been going to say was cut short by the precipitous entry of a pretty young theatre nurse, whose only sign of surprise at finding the surgeon bending passionately over a nursing Sister in the female changing room was a sliding sidelong look of conspiracy directed at Alison. Then the brown eyes went roguishly to Steve.

'Sister McCully's looking for you, Mr Barratt,' she simpered, wrinkling her pert nose attractively at him.

Alison had made things a thousand times worse for herself by guiltily jumping backwards and flushing to the roots of her fine fair hair. Unable to think of anything reasonably intelligent to say, and nothing whatsoever that would wipe the smirk from the girl's face, she made for the exit door. The story would be all over the hospital by nightfall, and she hardly imagined that it would flatter her. Only that Steve Barratt had scored again. But one thing she did know. It would be the last time he ever succeeded in putting her in a compromising position. The very last time.

CHAPTER THREE

IT WAS still early in the morning when Alison climbed out of the car to open the farm gate. There had been rain earlier on, but now a breeze was rustling through the clumps of silvery toi-toi growing in the ditch, mingling the smell of soaking vegetation with the sharp tang of the sea. From the hills came a long low whistle, and she looked up, shading her eyes against the glare of the sun. It took several moments to locate her uncle, and then she saw him herding a small flock of sheep near the bush-line. She watched the dogs circling to pick up the stragglers until they were out of sight, then she got back into the car and drove up the sandy road to the homestead.

Arthur the cat was sitting on the gatepost, a greedy eye trained on the goldfinch nest in the old totara tree. Alison left her car by the barn, giving the cat's ears a rub and telling him to be good as she let herself in at the gate. Her aunt was at the sink washing the breakfast dishes as she rounded the back of the house.

'Mum . . . it's Alison!' called a voice from the orchard, and Sue-Ann dropped out of a plum tree, giggling. She scrambled to her feet and came running across the lawn. Aunty May stepped out of the house, wiping soap bubbles from her arms.

'Alison love, we hoped you'd get here early,' she cried, warmly kissing her niece on the cheek.

'Hello, Aunty. Oh . . . Sue-Ann, what beautiful plums,' Alison exclaimed, as the girl shelled the dusky purple fruit from her pockets. 'I've never seen such a vivid shade.'

'Neither have I.' May permitted herself a rueful glance at the lurid voilet streaks in Sue-Ann's hair. 'Run and put the kettle on, there's a love.' She gazed after the girl, shaking her head. 'What ever will they think of next?'

Alison laughed. 'I'm so used to seeing hair every colour imaginable, I must confess I never gave it a thought.' She followed her aunt up the back steps and through the scullery and into the old-fashioned kitchen. 'I saw Uncle Henry up on the hill when I stopped by the gate. Twins not with him today?'

'They're over at the McCully farm helping with the sheep dipping,' Sue-Ann said, emerging from the pantry with a large cake-tin in her hands. 'Mum, can't I go? You said yesterday I could, an' Alison won't mind. You know the two of you like a good old chin-wag when I'm not around.'

As her aunt was still looking dubious, Alison said, smiling, 'I wouldn't be in the least offended, if Sue-Ann has something else she wants to do.'

'Oh well, seeing Alison will be staying the weekend, you might as well if you want. But Sue-Ann, I want you home by afternoon. No disappearing into town with your friends for the rest of the day.'

'Oh, Mum . . . 'Bye!' Sue-Ann buzzed them both on the cheek and raced out of the kitchen. May gave a resigned sign and turned her attention to the boiling kettle.

'Sit down, love, and tell me all about the hospital. Henry said you'd had an accident with the car.' May turned her head to study Alison with her soft worried eyes. 'He said it wasn't anything serious.'

'It wasn't,' Alison assured her. 'And the car is good as new. A nice man called Burt fixed it for me. I just twisted my ankle a bit and have to have physio and wear an elastic bandage for a while, but apart from that, there's no other damage.'

Her aunt placed the teapot on its brass stand on the table and set out large blue and white cups. 'All the same, it must have been a shock.' She passed the tea. 'Here you are, love. Now then, last time you were here, I remember you were all agog to meet the doctor on your ward. The one still on holiday, remember?'

'Oh . . . him.' Alison pulled a face—an expression of pain.

'What's he like?' May asked, surprised, and more than a little curious. Alison shrugged, anxious to get off the subject.

'Like any other arrogant young doctor who thinks he knows it all. He just needs keeping in his place. Don't worry, I can handle him.' And she went on to tell her aunt about the accident, quite neglecting to mention exactly who it was she could thank for rescuing her. Afterwards she helped May with the housework and then sat out on the scullery steps to shell peas picked fresh from the garden. It was pleasant and relaxing, listening to the still country sounds, the occasional baaing of sheep in the next paddock and the hens clucking as they scratched about in the orchard, the distant muffled bark of a dog.

'Hello, who's this? My lovely girl come to see me?' Uncle Henry came round the corner of the house with the two short-haired collies at his heels. Henry Prentice was as unlike her father as it was possible for a brother to be. Bluff and good-natured, he was content to live quietly and run his sheep over the land he had wrested from the bush during the twenty years he had been out from the Old Country—as England was still referred to. Looking at him, few of his neighbours would have guessed at his urban upbringing in a fashionable part of London, for like all New Zealand farmers, he wore a black sleeveless singlet, heavy twill trousers and hobnailed boots.

'Dinner's nearly ready,' May announced, emerging from the house. The farming community always had a huge cooked dinner at midday, and though Alison was unaccustomed to such, the salt air had made her ravenously hungry.

'Didn't I see Sue-Ann dodging off down the Bay road?' Henry asked. May frowned. The Bay road was in the opposite direction to Matepai, their neighbouring farm.

'I hope not. She said she was going over to the McCullys'. Irini is expecting her for a meal. But she did take her togs, so I expect she's gone for a dip on the way. There's a nice sandy beach not far from here,' she explained to Alison. 'We'll go after lunch, if you like, then I'll take you over and introduce you to Irini. I've baked some jam rolls—with all the extras on the place, she'll be glad of them.'

As they drove past the Matepai sheep yards that afternoon, the utility was hailed with whistles and shouts from the men. May's baking was second to none and her jam rolls were famous. Up at the house they found Irini buttering pikelets in the kitchen, a task May took over as soon as Alison had been warmly welcomed.

'Your Sue-Ann, she's been a real help to me today,' Irini said, as they were laying the long wooden table. Alison thought her aunt looked relieved to hear it.

Soon after, the boys came trailing in from the wash-house. The twins, Hugh and Charlie, beamed at Alison and shyly introduced her to the McCully boys. Frank arrived wiping his sinewy arms with a rough towel.

'Well now, and have you met my sister yet?' he asked Alison. And when she smilingly shook her head, he said, 'Ah well, you go along to the operating theatre and introduce yourself. The pair of you will get on fine.' He put an arm round his wife and the other round May and kissed them both. Then Irini poured the tea from her enormous pot and the mugs were handed round the table. Suddenly everybody was talking at once, all shyness forgotten. Alison looked round the table. The twins had inherited the Prentice family fairness and tendency to burn and freckle, whereas the McCully boys had taken after their beautiful mother, a direct descendant of a Maori chieftain in the still powerful Ngati-Whakaue tribe.

'Where's Sue-Ann?' asked May suddenly.

'Ah now, you go worrying about that girl too much, May,' Frank said. He had come out from Ireland at eleven years of age, and still spoke with a thick brogue. 'She went in with young Paddy in the Ute to get the hen mash. She'll be back soon—Paddy'll see to that.'

'That's all right, if she's with your Paddy,' May said quietly.

The weekend went much too quickly for Alison, Sunday passed with a family picnic at a scenic gorge, where the river ran deep and cool over smooth round stones through the bush-covered ravines. But at last it was time. Sunburned and happy, Alison waved to her aunt and uncle, the twins and Sue-Ann, and turned the Mini into the late afternoon sun, taking the Bay road back to Fort William. In a basket by her side nestled three jars of May's special plum jam. There was also an enormous sponge cake made with farm eggs and filled with whipped cream from the farm's own dairy.

She went on duty the next morning humming a tune, feeling relaxed and confident. At the duty room door she almost collided with Chris Laidlaw. 'Oh, what a night,' moaned the harassed night nurse. 'Hang on, be with you in a moment. There's coffee in the pot if you want it,' and she dashed off down the corridor.

Alison stared after her and began to feel less relaxed. But it was reassuring to see on the table outside the office a neat row of surgical gowns, each with its own covered bowl and pile of notes. By the look of it, Chris had the children prepared for morning theatre. That was the main thing, whatever else. Nothing upset a surgeon more than to have his list thrown out by some slip-up on the ward.

Chris joined her as Alison was pouring the coffee. 'They've eaten, every one of them,' she said grimly. Alison's hand wavered.

'For a moment I thought you were trying to tell me the pre-ops had eaten,' she said with a strangled laugh, which died quickly. 'Don't tell me they have?'

Chris fell into a chair and closed her eyes. 'The twins had food stashed away. They and the five going down for their Ts and As this morning all had a feast. It happened about four, when I had my break. The student was in with the special nurse most of the time. They were having a hell of a time with young Billy, apparently. And then at five, little Sally rang for a vomit bowl. Poor little mite is as sick as a dog. She was first on the list, by the way.'

'I don't suppose Mr Barratt knows about this yet?' Alison sighed when Chris shook her head.

'He doesn't. He'll go beserk when he finds out all his patients on the morning list have to be cancelled.' Chris added gloomily, 'With good reason.'

Alison was nodding, trying to be objective about it, but

her feeling of well-being was evaporating fast. This was serious. She took a deep breath. There would be nothing for it but to tighten up on the rules, though there was no point in discussing it now. Chris looked whacked. She would have to see what could be done about getting more night staff. Their allocation was ridiculous. 'Let's have the report,' she said quietly, 'then you can get off and have a good sleep.'

'What a hope,' the night nurse muttered. 'We're having the kitchen re-done and the house will be overrun with great clumping men hammering at things.' With a long sigh she flipped open the report book and began.

When Chris had departed, Alison dialled Steve Barratt's home phone number. Over the weekend she had concentrated on keeping him out of her thoughts, and had discovered it was surprisingly difficult. Alison fussed with her veil, listening to the buzzing ring, distracted. Why didn't he answer? Had he left already? Was he in the shower? She had a mental picture of him dashing to the phone, wet, a towel draped round his waist. Perhaps he didn't live alone, she had never thought to ask. Well, he was so young, he probably lived with his family. But what if a woman's voice answered, and it wasn't his mother? Alison frowned, almost at the point of hanging up.

'Morning, Sister . . .' Alison jumped and swung round. Steve Barratt sauntered in. Did the man have to tippytoe about the place? She snatched a quick glance to see if he wasn't wearing trainers. No. The same highly polished shoes and spotlessly white socks; somewhere at the back of her mind she wondered who did his laundry. He stood looking at her, his hair still slightly damp, curling at the ends. The strong line of his jaw had that smooth, clean, gleaming, just shaved look.

'Who were you calling so early in the morning?'

'I—oh . . .' Alison dropped the receiver back into its place. 'You're very early,' she hedged, opening the night report. 'Ah, the coffee is still hot, if you'd like a cup.'

'No, thanks all the same. Busy morning in theatre—I thought I'd do a quick round, then buzz on down.' His grin was wicked. He'd met Chris on the way out and heard the whole story from her, but he was looking forward to hearing it from Miss Efficiency herself. Since the day he had kissed her, she had avoided him like the plague. He figured she wanted to forget it ever happened—and that was just fine with him. She wasn't in much danger of it happening again either. As far as Steve was concerned, it was just one of those things. Girls didn't usually object so strenuously to a little kiss.

'Well, I'm sorry,' mumbled Alison, 'but it might not be as busy as you expected.'

She was looking so charmingly upset—all anxious eyes and with a sunburnt nose she had tried to hide with a smudge of powder—Steve relented. 'It's OK, I know what happened.' He picked up the pot and poured himself a mug of coffee. Alison was staring at him.

'You know? Why didn't you say?' she asked, puzzled, making him feel guilty for keeping her on the rack when she was so obviously worried about having to tell him. Steve didn't like being made to feel guilty, and he shrugged irritably.

'I really am sorry,' Alison said, with a helpless gesture. 'Of course I accept full responsibility and I'll take steps to see it never happens again. But what can we do now? Is there any chance of getting them to theatre this afternoon?'

Steve shook his head.

'Not a chance in hell. Theatres are fully booked. Though maybe tomorrow, if I go and prostrate myself at McCully's feet. Damned shame, I don't like keeping kids in an extra day, or two, or three. How on earth did they get their mits on the food in the first place? I thought you had some infallible scheme for preventing it.'

'I thought so too.' Alison frowned, thinking of the memo she had studied over the weekend which outlined the changes the new Matron hoped to bring about. 'I want more well trained,' she laid an emphasis on the two words, 'qualified staff, but with the general relaxation in all areas of training, I'm very much afraid I'm not going to get them.' Steve put down his cup, he wasn't in any mood to start discussing it.

'I'd better take a look at the one who was sick before the

morning staff get here to claim your attention.' The old edge of dislike was back in his voice and Alison felt sorry she had mentioned the new proposals, though they were going to have to be discussed, and discussed thoroughly at some point. He had been surprisingly nice, though—she had been expecting he would blow his top. Most surgeons would have.

'Yes, certainly,' she said swiftly. 'Come with me.' She walked briskly ahead of him down the ward, her starched veil fluttering out behind in a stiff V. Steve wondered how she managed to keep the thing on.

In this early hour, most of the children were still sleeping, the terrors of the night well behind them, a new unknown day yet to be faced without the comfort of home and mum and brothers and sisters. Some were awake, though, and watched incuriously from wide eyes, a favourite object stuffed against a button nose. Alison stopped by a bed that should have had a child tucked within its pristine covers. There was in fact only an untidy mound of blankets.

'She must have gone to the bathroom—I'll just go and fetch her.' Alison quickly did a tour of the toilets and bathrooms, then the sluice room, the store room then checked the outside play area. But no, the doors were still locked from the inside. Oh God, where was she? It wasn't unheard of, to have a child go missing from the ward, and Alison had a sticky feeling that anything was likely this morning. In a series of brief flashes, she saw the child wandering alone on to the road outside the hospital, cars swerving to avoid her. Oh, dear God! Because she could have followed the night staff out through the ward doors and slipped away.

She hurried back up the ward, searching as she went. Steve Barratt had apparently given them up, for he too had gone. Probably for breakfast, Alison thought sourly. By the time she got to the kitchen she was frantic. Never again would she let the night nurse go without first doing a round and making sure she had the children all accounted for. Finally she went back to the office to raise the general alarm.

Steve Barratt was settled comfortably in a chair, Sally on his knee. 'Look who I found,' he said, his cheerfulness grating on Alison's ears.

'I've been looking everywhere for her,' Alison said, quietly stressing every word. The child certainly looked sick, her face was the shade of cheap white blotting paper.

'She was visiting the side rooms—weren't you, Sally? You were gone so long, I went on a search of my own.' His eyes were on Alison's face. 'Ever see a case of German measles, Sister?' he asked drily.

Alison blinked, and peered at the pale face. Sure enough, there was the faintest rash of minute pink spots, hands and arms as well. 'Oh lord,' she said under her breath, then said, knowing it was like shutting the stable door after the horse had bolted, 'We'll have to isolate her.'

'Leave her in the ward,' Steve suggested mildly. 'Best age for kids to have German measles.'

Alison knew all about the theory, it had its points, and she preferred not to have to nurse a ward through a raging epidemic of measles. 'Let's get Sally back to bed, shall we? We'll discuss it later.' Sally wasn't prepared to be brushed off so easily, after gaining the santuary of the office where she was enjoying being the focus of attention, and Steve had to persuade her with bribes before she consented to stay in her own bed. Afterwards he joined Alison at the wash-basin. 'How d'you manage to keep them in bed?' he asked, a trifle tetchily. Alison had to suppress a smile.

'You'll have to change your coat,' she said, with a quick sideways glance. She dried her hands carefully. 'We simply have to isolate her, we can't risk not doing so.'

'Why not? Save them all having to be vaccinated later on, and with an incubation of fourteen to nineteen days, she's already done a pretty fair job of spreading the infection.'

'Quarantine is twenty-one days,' Alison said crisply. 'Sally should be isolated until the rash disappears.' Steve glowered at her, not that Alison took a whit of notice. 'Look,' she said, appealing to him, 'parents don't send in their children to contract German measles. They can take the kind of risk you're suggesting, but we can't. We mustn't. It's our duty to prevent an epidemic.'

'What do you want me to do?' Steve asked finally. 'Send all the children home?' Was he being sarcastic? She gave him a quick look and decided to ignore it.

'The Ts and As will have to be sent home, and quarantined, if their parents make that decision. And the twins too. They had most contact with Sally, apparently. Little monkeys—they had the food hidden and they're always up to some mischief.'

'They can go home,' Steve said shortly. 'I looked at the lab reports last night, they're both clear.' He threw a bunch of paper towels into the disposal unit, frowning. He didn't have much choice with the kids on this morning's list. He couldn't operate, and he had no idea when he could get them rescheduled. No sense in keeping them in to get measles.

'And Sally?' Alison asked. God, she was persistent, Steve thought.

'Quarantine her,' he said, after a heavy moment. 'What about Rosa? She's in the next bed to Sally.' He turned a quizzical brow on her, wondering how she was going to work that one out.

Immediately she looked at him, uncertain, worried. Rosa was an eighteen-month-old, a child whose dislocated hips had gone unnoticed at birth. Now, at walking age, she was having to spend a year in hospital with her legs abducted in a frog plaster. Life was difficult enough for her, without the added misery of measles.

'She'd fret terribly being shut away in a side room. No, no, she'll have to stay where she is. Let's just hope she escapes. Can you imagine having a rash under all that plaster?' Alison was frowning, preoccupied. Her face took on a soft defenceless look which didn't escape Steve. She had got him to accede to her wishes, but she wasn't crowing about it. There was none of the bloody-mindedness he often associated with her father.

'I'd better go and give the report,' Alison said, noticing that the morning staff had arrived. 'And we'd better all brush up on our aseptic technique,' she said grimly, sounding rather more like the Sister he expected her to be.

'Nurse Te Atawhai . . .' Hine pulled up short in the corridor as Sister Prentice rapped out her name. Alison had been to lunch. Coming back across the lawn, she had been astounded to see a horse tethered to the fence in the children's play area. 'What's that horse doing there?' she asked sharply.

'It's all right, Sister, she's used to children, they won't bother her none.'

'That's hardly the point . . .' Alison made an effort to keep calm. 'I wasn't thinking of the horse, Nurse, it's the children I'm worried about. What if it kicks, or—or treads on one of them? How did it get there?'

'Her name's Bess,' Hine said with the note of sulky truculence Alison found so irritating. At that moment Jenny Duncan popped her head out of a side room door.

'Hine, I'm waiting for those charts . . . Oh, sorry, Sister.'

'Never mind, Staff. Just tell me what's going on.' Jenny emerged from the room and Hine disappeared inside with a roll of her eyes.

'Rangi King's been admitted. He's been in before. His family live on Keina Island—you know, the one you can get to across the mud flats at low tide.' Alison nodded impatiently. 'Rangi's dad brought him over on Bess. Had to swim her.'

'What's Rangi in for?' asked Alison, keeping a wary eye on Bess through the window.

'Pneumonia. Same as always,' Jenny said, sounding quite unconcerned. Alison thought she must be hearing things. How could anyone bring an ill child through sea water on the back of a horse? 'Dr McKenzie's seeing him now, Sister.'

'Jenny, I'm terrified the children will get trampled on.' Alison turned from the window. 'Where's Rangi's father?'

'Well . . .' Jenny made an apologetic face, 'he's gone off visiting somewhere. Hine will know probably, if you want him, but he usually turns up before too long. Before dark anyway. That's why he leaves Bess in the play area. It's the shadiest place. The kids love her.'

'Well, she can't stay there,' Alison snapped. 'She only has to lift one of those great hooves.' Alison could see herself explaining to astounded parents why their only child—admitted with earache and entrusted to her care—was now being treated for crush injuries. She felt drained, the muggy heat of the day, the complacency of just about everyone she met—was no one worried? Did it always have to be her who insisted, ordered, nagged . . .

'Ask Hine to come out,' Alison said finally, mentally taking a tighter grip on herself. 'She can at least tether the animal to the other side of the fence—and I don't want to hear one word about there not being enough shade.' Checking her watch, she added, 'You should have been away to lunch ages ago, Staff Nurse. Staff Manning was to relieve you.'

'Oh well, there was something special Clair wanted to do, so I had a bite in the kitchen,' Jenny said, before realising what she had let slip. She knew, as well as Alison, it was against the rules to eat on the ward. But everybody did.

'I don't think I heard that,' Alison murmured, a glint of humour appearing in her eyes. She had done it too often in the past, herself. She glanced at her watch again. 'I've got a few tedious jobs to catch up on, then I'll look in on Rangi when he's settled.' So saying, she made a beeline for the office. What with one thing and another, she hadn't been near her desk all morning, and if she didn't get the order forms made out they would be out of linen this time tomorrow. Alison paused just long enough to see that Hine did as she had asked, and gave a sigh of relief when she saw Bess installed on the other side of the fence. True, there wasn't as much shade. On the other hand, it was beginning to cloud over. She wouldn't want to think of the poor horse being left to suffer under the hot sun all afternoon.

With her mind at ease, Alison settled down to work. Normally she had no trouble concentrating, but when she found she had filled in a request for disposable gowns twice over, she stopped with a vexed sigh. It was warm in the office. A fly buzzed at the window, the fan whirred sleepily, stirring the sluggish air. Alison propped her chin on the palm of her hand. What was happening to her? She was moody. One moment she had everything at her fingertips, the next, she was dreamy and forgetful. That wasn't like her. Worse were the thoughts that came in a clear sequence late at night. Passionate, tender, raging thoughts that had to do with one man and the way he had kissed her. She had tried to block them off, but how could she? They kept coming back and she found herself dreaming, hoping, regretting . . .

Her inner restlessness provoked a sense of conflict and brought her to her feet. She went to the window and flung it open wide. The air was fragrant with the intoxicating scent of summer roses, the echoes from a nearby school drifted across the grassy slopes, a music lesson, children singing.

For heaven's sake—she had to get rid of this curious lethargy. Obliterate it. Get rid of her fantasy. There was only jagged-edged reality. The man would kiss any woman who was halfway attractive and with whom he found himself alone. What was more, she expected a good many nurses had, at one time or another, fancied themselves as Mrs Steve Barratt. She had no intention of falling into that old trap. Mooning over the roses indeed! She was working diligently at her desk when Molly burst headlong through the door.

'Rosa's choking. She swallowed something and it's blocking her airway.' Alison was up in a flash.

'Dr McKenzie,' she asked the frantic nurse, 'is he still in the ward?'

'No,' wailed Molly. 'He left ages ago.' Alison shot past her. Jenny Duncan was emerging from the side room with a kidney dish in her hand.

'Leave that and bring the trachy tray,' Alison called to her, and then she ran.

Several nurses surrounded the bed. Rosa was a thoroughly alarming shade of purple. One nurse was holding a teddy bear. 'Look, she must have swallowed a glass eye.' Alison glanced at the bear's remaining eye and decided it was exactly the right size to lodge in the larynx and block off the trachea. As Jenny came up, she grabbed the tray.

'Get the team up from theatre.' Her voice was terse. She ripped the covers from the tray, snapped on surgical gloves and nodded to one of the nurses. 'Pour me some iodine in the gallipot.' To Molly she gave rapid instructions.

'Extend Rosa's head back on the pillows . . . That's the way, gently. Keep talking to her . . .' Pale as a ghost, Molly did exactly as she was told. The other nurses held the child's hands.

Quickly, Alison swabbed Rosa's throat and administered a local anaesthetic. Then, drawing a deep breath, she picked up the scalpel and slid the blade into place. Feeling for the larynx with her gloved fingers, she made a small traverse incision below the first tracheal ring. A trickle of blood oozed out, she pressed with a swab, with her other hand she grabbed a tracheostomy tube and inserted it. Almost at once there was a satisfying gulp of air. Rosa, recovering rapidly, opened her mouth to suck in enough breath to howl.

Only then did Alison's hand begin to shake. She had never been called on to do a tracheostomy, and she blessed the surgeon at her old training school who had insisted his students knew how. 'Anyone who works with children,' he had said, 'must be able to do an emergency tracheostomy if the situation arises. On the kitchen table with the carving knife, if necessary, but do it. Remember, it may be the only thing that can save that child's life.'

But had she done it properly? If the incision was made in the wrong place all sorts of difficulties could occur. It was then she felt Steve Barratt's hand, warm and strong on her arm.

'Good girl,' she heard him whisper softly, and felt almost faint with relief.

Steve put on gloves and bending down, gently probled the airway into a secure position and rapidly tied the tapes. Rosa was still in such a state of shock at having had her supply of air abruptly cut off and then miraculously restored again, she allowed Steve to fiddle around without protest, the local anaesthetic numbing the pain she would normally have felt. By the time the anaesthetist arrived, her colour was retuning to a healthy shade of pink. Alison ruefully indicated the teddy bear and the one vacant eye. He looked very forlorn.

'Where did you learn to do that?' the doctor asked, surveying Alison's handiwork.

'Told you she was top-notch,' Steve said, his casual words sending Alison's heart leaping. He peeled off his gloves and told her in a low aside, 'We'll take Rosa straight down to theatre and get the foreign body out under general.' Rosa knew all about being taken for rides in her bed and she didn't like it, she was apt to scream if anyone should so much as move the bed an inch. 'Can you tee it up with Sister McCully and let her know we'll be down in about ten minutes. You think we can get her sedated in that time?' Steve asked, glancing at Rosa's puckered mouth.

'Think so,' Alison said, smiling. Rosa was only a baby, but she definitely knew her rights, and anything she didn't like the look of, she let everybody know.

'When did she last eat?' the anaesthetist was asking.

'Lunch time. Twelve midday.' Alison looked at Molly, who had fed Rosa. 'She ate everything, didn't she?'

'Every scrap,' Molly assured him. Alison had been on to her about allowing the children dessert before the first course was finished, and she had coaxed Rosa to eat every bit. She beamed, feeling proud of herself.

'Great,' the anaesthetist muttered sourly. 'Just my luck,' and a demoralised Molly gave Alison a can't-win-whatever-I-do look.

'We're going to have to prepare a side room,' Alison said to Jenny Duncan, after Rosa had gone down. 'She'll need specialling for the next twenty-four hours if they leave the trachy in. And they will, if there's any swelling. She has to be able to breathe on her own without any distress. Billy can come back into the ward, I think, Rosa can have his room.' Clair Manning had come into the office and she stood twiddling her fob watch.

'Mind if I go off half an hour earlier this afternoon? My mother isn't very well . . .' She allowed this statement to hang in mid-air.

'Oh, but of course.' Alison was immediately sympathetic. 'You can go soon as you hand over. Let me see . . .' She ran an eye over the roster to see who would be in charge of the end Billy was being returned to. 'I do hope there's nothing seriously wrong . . .' She glanced up at the Staff Nurse.

'No, just a bad dose of 'flu,' Clair murmured, not quite looking Alison in the eye.

By the time Rosa was back from Theatre, the change-over had been completed and the morning staff had gone. Alison wasn't due off for another hour. Though she had been on before the morning shift arrived at seven, it was her own decision. Officially, she didn't have to start until eight. But Alison liked to take the report from the night nurse, especially when she had been away from the ward for two days. Besides, she liked coming into the hospital when it was quiet and the children were still sleeping and everything was peaceful. There was something special about that hour.

'Hello.' Rob McKenzie appeared at the office door. 'Everything OK? We left the tracheostomy tube in for the time being. Not for long. You did a pretty good job. Teddy's got his eye back in.'

'I saw that,' Alison said, smiling. 'I think we should send all the toys down to have their spare parts sutured on. Somebody did a thorough job?'

'Thank Steve. It took him longer to sew the eye back on the teddy than it did to fish it out of Rosa's larynx.' Alison visualised the scene in her mind. There was a lot of good in the man—in anyone who would take the time to sew the eye back on a child's teddy, and he would do it with the same air of control he did everything. Vaguely she became aware that Rob was saying something.

'I'm sorry, Rob. I-I was thinking about something else. You were saying?'

'I was just wondering if you wouldn't mind doing a quick round. There's a few things Steve asked me to check up on. Oh, and he wants me to look at Emma Fairchild's lab reports if they're back.' Alison stared at him in surprise. Steve always made a point of doing a round before leaving the hospital late afternoon and she had come to expect it as part of the routine. Rob grinned. 'All right for some,' he said.

'How do you mean?' Alison asked, very keen suddenly to know what was so important that it had kept Steve Barratt from a well established custom.

'By the look of it he and Clair are off for a picnic.' He laughed. 'I saw them getting into the Land Rover with all the beach gear, hamper, cooler, the lot. They've got a nice evening for it. If this weather keeps up, we'll have our barbecue tomorrow night. You're still coming?'

'What . . . Oh yes, Rob. I hadn't forgotten, thanks.' She turned away and gathered up the folders, as carefully as a child entrusted with an unfamiliar task.

'Shall we start with Rosa? And I'd like you to see Billy, he's in the ward now, you know. Seems quite happy. Oh, and of course, there's little Sally.' Alison gave a strange little laugh. 'You know, I'm beginning to see spots now. I keep peering at every child I see. But there doesn't seem to be any others coming down with the measles. Yet anyway.'

Funny, it wasn't Clair's lame excuse about a sick mother that hurt. It was the thought of Steve and Clair together. And that was ridiculous when the two of them were practically engaged. What was she thinking about?

It was stupid to mind so much. But even more stupid to find out she minded at all.

CHAPTER FOUR

ALISON sat with baby Elizabeth Jane on her lap, and kept a restraining hand on two-year-old Jamie who wanted to investigate the decidedly more interesting developments around the barbecue pit. It was beyond Alison how Rob's pretty young wife Dorothy remained sweet-tempered and patient, with four children under school age and a bizarre collection of pets seemingly always underfoot. Frustrated in his efforts to explore, Jamie sat down and began to howl and was immediately offered a chocolate biscuit by the three-year-old, a pink-cheeked sprite who had stared unwaveringly at Alison, but who had not yet been tempted to speak despite considerable prompting from her parents.

'Don't let him get chocolate on your lovely dress,' called Dorothy, the warning coming too late, however, Jamie having decided at that moment to bury his face in the soft folds of Alison's skirt.

'Don't worry, I've had it for ages,' Alison lied cheerfully. It was silly anyway to have worn a delicate silk dress in palest apricot to a family barbecue. But it had been sitting in her wardrobe, and goodness knows, there was little opportunity for her to wear it, though she hadn't bargained for this evening being quite so casual. She settled the baby comfortably against her shoulder—and then felt an ominous trickle of damp down her back.

'Bubby's been sick,' the three-year-old informed her mother in a piping clear voice, then resettled her relentless gaze back on Alison's face.

When Alison had been mopped and sponged, the baby and the two youngest tucked up in bed for the night, and they were once again assembled on the lawn, Rob introduced a new guest. 'Alison, I want you to meet Trevor Smaille. He's on the Hospital Board, but don't let that put you off,' this last being said with a wink and a nudge. Alison found herself shaking hands with a mild-eyed stocky young man with thinning hair. They exchanged a few pleasantries, and then Bob said it was time to eat, and where was Steve.

Alison paused, looking at him. 'I didn't know Steve Barratt was coming.'

'She sees enough of us at the hospital, poor girl,' Rob explained to Trevor, and Alison realised then what her voice must have conveyed, unerring barometer that it was. Rob dragged one of the dogs away from the table and shouted for his son to come and tie him up before the food got devoured.

In the confusion, Steve had arrived. He wore a blue polo shirt and a pair of khakis faded almost white and a pair of sneakers with blue strips. His tanned face was smiling. He was so fresh and clean Alison was suddenly conscious that she looked anything but, with her stained, crushed skirt, and the decidedly unattractive sour milk smell clinging to her.

Steve wasn't expecting Alison, Rob had said nothing to him about inviting her. He would have made some excuse and backed out, if he had known. Yesterday she had seemed almost friendly, approachable at least—though she had probably forced herself, seeing it was the ward's fault his list had been cancelled—but it hadn't been the case today; despite his attempts to jolly her along she had remained politely frozen. He had concluded that she was obviously too uptight to respond to any attempt at friendship. He caught Dorothy around the waist and gave her an affectionate kiss, laughing at some remark she passed and sniffing the air appreciatively. Dot's honey-glazed chicken was worth an uncomfortable evening, even though Rob liked to take all the credit for cooking it and would stand for ages turning it this way and that over his charcoal grill.

Steve accepted a glass of wine and politely nodded in Alison's direction. He knew who Trevor Smaille was, of course, and wondered what had induced Rob and Dot to invite the man. He did nothing but argue about hospital policy, taking everything from the narrow, petty bureaucratic view point of a small town accountant. He felt even more annoyed to see him listening with avid interest to Alison. Steve hoped she wasn't trotting out all the state secrets, it would be just like Smaille to pump her. Next thing, there would be a meeting about some piffling thing that didn't matter a tinker's cuss, and then the usual deluge of memos, the Board respectfully pointing out such and such. Always playing politics, nothing better to do. He wandered over.

'Steve . . . Good to see you.' The thin mouth smiled and the voice held the right mixture of cordial interest, but the eyes retained their careful scrutiny. He was an inquisitive guy all right. Steve supposed he would be running for mayor any day.

For a second—no more—Steve's mobile face froze, then he said easily, 'Sorry to keep everyone waiting.' He couldn't help but notice how different Alison looked in the soft, filmy thing she was wearing, or the way her hair tumbled down her back in a shining fall. It occurred to him then that perhaps she had come with Smaille. Though why that should irritate him even more, he didn't know. They were probably suited to each other. Smaille might even solve the problem by marrying her. If he did, it would be a thorn out of his side.

'Nothing wrong, is there? At the hospital, I mean.' Alison thought that perhaps there had been trouble with Rosa's tracheostomy tube—they could be tricky at times. Her eyes studied him anxiously.

'No, nothing in your department,' he smiled as an act of courtesy before glancing over her head at Rob. 'Suzie turned up at the house as I was leaving. Remember her?'

Rob considered the question as he turned the chicken. 'Oh yeah, sure I remember,' he said, laughing in the easy way men have of doing when discussing an old girlfriend.

'Well, that's why I'm late,' Steve said, grinning hugely. Pity they couldn't all share the joke, Alison thought. And good luck to Suzie, because Clair wasn't the sort of girl who would move over easily. Rob was neglecting the chicken and the marinade was sizzling on the hot coals and producing an alarming curl of blue smoke. Suzie, whoever she was, must be something else, Alison decided.

Eventually dinner was served on a trestle table set up under a beautiful tree with broad gleaming leaves and clusters of yellow fruit. Alison admired it and Trevor Smaille was ready to impart its name and history, claiming it had been brought out from Europe with the first settlers. Steve disagreed and said it was a karaka tree and native to New Zealand. From then on the feeling of discord between the two men was more pronounced.

They had been invited to take their own places at the table. Steve had chosen to sit on the side directly opposite Alison, which meant that she had to carefully avoid his eyes and it made her uncomfortable because she had an insistent feeling he was observing her. For a while the talk was about the weather and the likelihood of the summer continuing hot and dry, but inevitably the conversation turned to the hospital.

'Tell us how the meeting went today,' Rob said, returning to the table with yet another platter of barbecued chicken.

'What meeting was that?' Trevor was quick to ask. He helped himself to several more pieces, licking his fingers in the process.

'Matron was just outlining a few of the changes she had in mind for the children's ward,' Alison said. She thought that Trevor was sitting rather more closely to her on the long wooden bench than was strictly necessary, and it occurred to her that she didn't like him particularly. Though compared with the intensity of her dislike for Steve Barratt, it scarcely mattered.

Trevor made a rueful face and leaned closer. 'I heard she's full of outlandish ideas.' His tone reeked of a sickening complicity, and Alison frowned.

'Oh, I wouldn't call them outlandish at all,' she found herself responding sharply. 'You mustn't forget that many of her ideas are at an experimental stage. Some may not be practical for a conventional unit such as we have at the moment, but they're certainly worth considering for the new wing.' She was talking eagerly, her face alight. 'I read her notes for bridging the gap between the hospital and Maori community and found them very refreshing. Someone is really thinking . . .' She came to a full stop—that someone was Steve Barratt, he was the instigator, the one behind Matron's radical approach—and she had been talking much too much. She met the alert blue eyes opposite. God in heaven, what had she said?

'Interesting,' he murmured, rubbing his chin meditatively and scarcely able to contain his amusement at finding Alison in his camp. He hadn't said a thing in its defence, hadn't needed to. She had said it all for him. Could it be she was prepared to give his schemes an innings after all?

Trevor Smaille dabbed at his lips with a greasy napkin and launched into a monologue about the foolhardiness of disrupting tried and tested methods and making a lot about how unattractive and untidy the hospital would look if the nurses were allowed to wear their own clothes, and so on.

On the point of nurses wearing mufti, and as he seemed to be addressing her, Alison commented, 'It would only be in the children's ward, and as that's at the back of the hospital hardly anyone would notice.'

Steve was laughing quietly. 'You have to admit there's a certain logic to that,' he told a perplexed Trevor Smaille, who had begun to wonder if Alison wasn't taking the micky out of him.

'I don't think it matters where you're situated in geographical terms,' he stated humourlessly. Alison said nothing, she had said too much as it was, and a nervousness, a vague discomfort, accompanied the recognition of it.

The eyes under the extraordinarily grave brows deepened with the lengthening shadows. Steve had never known eyes that could change so with mood and light. They were troubled now, and he thought he knew the reason. She was interested in the new ideas all right. But she didn't want to be pushed and bullied into anything she hadn't quite accepted. Had her father tried to push her too hard? he wondered, studying her covertly through a curl of cigar smoke. She could be stubborn.

'Nothing has been settled yet,' he heard himself telling Smaille, his eyes still resting on Alison. 'And certainly won't be. Not without the full support of all parties concerned. There'll be no arbitrary decisions.'

Alison glanced up, surprised. After her little speech, she was expecting to be railroaded into making a commitment—and she felt unable to do that at the moment; there were areas she couldn't agree on, yet anyway. For the very first time, she felt he understood her position, and was prepared to listen. She felt she could trust him. More than that, she was aware of an interest in him that was outside all professional concern, and she knew it was going to be difficult to rationalise away, just as certainly as she knew it would bring her pain.

'I really must be going,' Alison said regretfully after everyone had been sitting over their coffee for almost an hour. Whether it had been the convivial atmosphere that had prevailed since the conversation had ceased to be about politics, or the wine, or a combination of both, Alison didn't know. But she did know that she felt relaxed and happy and loath to make the first move. Trevor Smaille leapt to his feet.

'Let me see you home.' As his hand closed possessively on her arm, Alison was already smiling and shaking her head, saying she had her own car. And then, after all the farewells had been made, and the promises to visit again very soon, her car wouldn't start. Alison tried the ignition key again and waited for the reassuring rumble. Nothing. Glancing anxiously at the dashboard, she tried again.

'Trouble?' Steve Barrett rested his hands lightly on the car roof and leaned down.

'Nothing seems to work,' Alison said nervously. 'Do you think it could be something electrical?'

'Move over and let's see what I can do.' Steve opened the door, preparing to swing his big elegant body into the quite ridiculously small seat. Alison hastily vacated her place for the passenger's seat. 'Don't suppose you have a flash-light . . . Oh, you do.' He fiddled about behind the dash for a few minutes while she held the torch.

'No loose wires far as I can see. Hang on, I'll take a look under the bonnet.' He was back within a very short time.

'Looks like you'll have to be my passenger tonight.' Alison felt her stomach contract in the mixture of excitement and apprehension someone must feel when they are skating on ice known to be dangerously thin in places. Steve casually opened the door for her to get out.

'Oh . . .' Alison tried to think of a dozen excuses. 'You don't think, if I were to get a push, it would start?' Nevertheless, she had climbed out, and was staring up at him. He looked very tall and calm and orderly. He had the quality some men have, that beckoned, and women simply left what they were doing to follow.

'Probably not,' Steve said with a grin. He was thinking that his offer could have been rather more graciously accepted, and suspected she was worried about the long drive home. He remembered that he had forced his attentions on her the last time they were alone. As soon as they were on the road, he apologised. He thought it was the least he could do.

'I owe it to you, I think. It was unforgivable of me, and whatever you may think, I'm not in the habit of going around kissing attractive ladies.' He glanced at her. 'Well, not on duty, anyway.' It hadn't been his intention to raise the matter again, but he could hardly have her thinking he was some kind of sex maniac.

Oh lord, if he was going to be nice, just when her defences were begining to crumble. 'Please,' Alison gave a light little laugh. 'I'd already put it out of my mind.'

Steve glanced at her sharply. She made it sound very easy to do, he thought, needled that she had apparently taken so little account of a kiss that had shaken him to his roots. Still, he shrugged, looking back at the road, he felt better for having brought the thing out into the open. Now he could forget it completely.

'Though I did wonder at the time how you could forget Clair so easily,' Alison said, causing him to frown.

'You don't believe all the hospital gossip, do you? We're

not engaged to each other, and probably never will be. Friends, that's all.' Alison wondered if Clair felt the same way, but she couldn't quite control a small, curious excitement that came with the knowledge that he wasn't contemplating marriage. Not just yet anyway. Or so he said. She fixed her eyes on the moth-spattered windscreen and wondered who Suzie was. As the silence lengthened between them, she felt constrained to ask.

'Suzie?' He shook his head. 'Young girl I've had rather a lot to do with one way and another over the years. I saw her first when I was still a medical student. She'd been farmed out to a few foster-parents by then. She was a difficult child, hyperactive, terrible nightmares and prone to screaming tantrums, so it wasn't surprising that she didn't stay very long with any one of them. Then at last she was settled with an elderly couple who were absolutely marvellous to her—liberal, open-minded, tolerant. Well, she seemed to be thriving, and then the foster-mother died. Suzie was seven by this time. Eventually she went to live with a family, it appeared to be working out and they were allowed to adopt her.'

'How did that turn out?' Alison asked, watching his face and sensing a compassion behind the matter-of-fact words she would never have guessed at. It was the quality, she realised now, that saved his face from being merely too handsome.

'The welfare people would call them suitable,' he said shortly, 'which means that probably I would not. I've never met them, but from what I gathered from Suzie, I'd say they were quite unsuited to bringing up a teenager of her temperament. All they seem to want is for her to toe the line, conform to their stereotype of what a daughter should be. You know the sort.' He glanced across at her. He liked a woman who could listen. Especially one who could do it without constantly fidgeting or fussing with her hair. Talking to Clair at times was like talking to himself, or a chit-chat machine. She would be primping her hair and peering into a mirror fixing her make-up, then she would ask him some totally irrelevant thing that had nothing whatsoever to do with what had been said beforehand. He grinned. Alison was all right.

'She turned up out of the blue this evening, having persuaded a neighbour to drive her out to see me, and spend an hour complaining how her mother wants her to stay home the whole time baking scones. So now you know about Suzie. And here we are, almost at your gate.'

Alison peered out and saw a light through the cabbage trees. She wondered if she should invite him in for a drink. It seemed churlish not to offer, though it was very late. She gave a happy little sigh. How quickly and pleasantly the evening had passed.

'Thank you for driving me back . . .' She hesitated. 'Would you like to come in?'

'Can I take a rain-check on that?' His eyes were smiling, questioning, as if there was going to be a next time. 'I'm going to see you to the door, though.' He pulled the brake lever up and clambered out. Alison got out and stood waiting for him, holding her bare arms, her heart beating just a little faster.

There was a heavenly stillness about the night and a stealing tide of perfume came from the verbena and lilac. Steve paused on the lawn and stood looking up at the sky. 'Look,' he said softly, turning her gently by the shoulders so she was looking in the right direction. 'You can see the Southern Cross.' Alison lifted her face to the winking stars, so cold and brilliant and unearthly in their purity. A different constellation from the one she had been born under.

James had proposed to her under the Northern Star, one high summer night when she had been intoxicated with the smell of English roses and English lavender, and terribly in love. She shivered a little in her wispy dress.

'Cold?' Steve asked, dropping his gaze to the top of her head, and for several seconds his fingers pressed more deeply into her soft shoulders.

'No.' Her voice was so quiet and so soft.

'Something walk over your grave?' He wondered what she was feeling, what her reflections were, or even if she was grieving; but instinctively guessing at the pain, yet knowing nothing of the dead summer or the memory of that other man in her background. She was so close, he could feel the sensual friction of her silk-sheathed, warm sweet body, sharpening his senses to a dangerous intensity.

She turned her face slightly, her eyes seemed to daydream, lips slightly parted, the pearls at her neck, soft and luminous in the starlight. Steve grew tense. In this dangerous tender mood he was just as likely to find himself kissing her again. For God's sake, he'd only just got around to apologising for the last time. She looked towards the house, staring at the roses climbing along the verandah, her shoulder just touching his chest.

'I must go in. Thank you.' He had to lean down to hear the soft words, then she was going. He watched her walk up the steps, womanly and graceful in her lovely dress. For a few seconds she was silhouetted in the lamplight as she paused briefly in the doorway to look back, then the door closed soundlessly.

Steve waited a moment, frowning in concentration, then he turned and strode back to the Land Rover. He had the road to himself for the rest of the way, which was perhaps a good thing, considering his driving was so wildly erratic.

Alison paused as she sorted the laboratory reports. 'We've got Emma Fairchild's microbiology results back.' She scanned the slip of paper anxiously, then waved it jubilantly in front of Jenny Duncan's nose. 'Look at that—negative. She'll be off antibiotics and home soon.' The phone rang as she was speaking and she picked it up still smiling. Everything was running smoothly for once, apart from the odd hiccup, and an unexpected drama when a child's pet mouse had been discovered, secreted in a toilet bag. But there seemed to be no more children coming down with measles, and despite getting in so late last night, she didn't feel in the least tired.

Suddenly the smile went from her face, she did a slow turn to look at Jenny. 'Yes,' she said, 'we can take them. Can you give me details?' For the next few minutes she wrote rapidly.

'We've got seven children coming in.' She put down the receiver slowly, her eyes on the notes. 'Five not badly hurt, probably concussion, and two with head injuries that sound serious, plus minor injuries. All girls. School bus ran off the road—brake failure, they think.' She glanced up at the wall map. 'Where's the Waimea Valley?'

Jenny found the place with a ruler. 'Doesn't look far, does it? But the roads are really bad. Who's bringing them in?'

'Ambulances from here, they've just gone out. The Waimea District MO is on the scene. That was the call we got over the car radio.' Alison got up and walked over to the board where the patients' names were slotted in. For a moment she studied it.

'The two serious cases can go into the side rooms nearest the office.' Picking out the cards, she juggled them around until she ended up with several spaces at the topmost end of the ward. 'The other five can go in here. They'll be on half-hourly neurological observations, so having them all in one place will be a help—make it a bit easier on the night nurse.' She bit at the end of her pencil, eyes narrowed in concentration. 'I'd better ring and see if we can get some extra staff for them. Who have we got on this afternoon, Jenny?'

The staff nurse ran rapidly through a list of names, Alison nodding every now and then. They were all good nurses, which was a blessing because they were in for a busy duty. Clair Manning had swopped her morning shift for the afternoon, so she would be in sole charge of the ward from the time Alison left until the night nurse came on.

About Clair's allegedly sick mother, Alison had kept silent. Sometimes things were not what they seemed. At the risk of seeming naive, Alison had given her the benefit of the doubt. In any case, she was a very good staff nurse who was capable of taking charge, and Alison recognised it.

'Heard the news, I see.' Steve wandered into the office. Did his loose-limbed rangy stride make her think it, wondered Alison, or was his lazy saunter a clever ploy to put others at their ease? If so, it was very effective. Jenny usually acted like a scared rabbit when someone in a white coat came upon her. But for Steve Barratt she had a glowing smile ready, and he never disappointed her. There was always a teasing compliment and a ready quip. Alison returned to her desk.

'We have. We're sorting out where to put them . . .' As she spoke she sorted charts and affixed stickers and the red dot which indicated which consultant the patient was admitted under. It had been so long since she had seen Gilbert Hains, the paediatric consultant, what with his extended holidays and fishing trips, she had almost forgotten what he looked like, but meanwhile and until he retired, he got his red dot.

Steve watched her collate a pile of charts. He liked the way she did things—calmly, methodically, no fuss, no panic. There were seven injured children on their way, and she might just have well been laying the table for afternoon tea. He had seen her moving around the ward, scooping up a fretful tot on the way to carry on her hip. Sometimes he had come into the office to find her rocking an infant in a pram while writing the report, serene, efficient, correct. He had never known a woman like her, the way she looked at him, eyes mildly appraising.

Hands discreetly clasped behind him, he turned to study the board. 'Can I help move the beds round for you?'

'Oh, would you?' Alison looked up smiling. Not many Registrars, however friendly, would make an offer like that. 'Thanks, that would be a great help. Jenny knows how I want them arranged, and who goes where.'

By the time the first ambulance drew up at the Accident and Emergency bay, the ward was standing ready. A little knot of anxious people had gathered, parents and family; they waited helplessly as the stretchers were rushed through the Casualty Department and along hushed corridors to the children's wing.

'Semi-comotosed, pupillary changes, motor paralysis, changes in pulse and respiration rate . . .' Alison stood by Steve Barratt in a darkened room as he went through a neurological examination.

'Let me have that torch again.' He directed the light on the child's left eye, then quickly swung the torch aside. The pupil remained fully dilated. Steve straightened up, frowning.

'Got the decadron?' Alison nodded and picked up a vial from the tray of emergency drugs. Swiftly she drew up the solution, flicking at the syringe with her finger to extract every last bubble of air. He nodded, and she swabbed the site, giving the injection with a quick expert jab.

'She'll need careful monitoring,' Steve said. He folded his stethoscope, stuffing it into his coat pocket. 'I'm not so worried about the little one next door, but this child . . . Cerebral oedema can result in intracranial hypertension. We have to know her rising and falling levels of consciousness and the recordings have to be accurate. Who'll be looking after her?' He gave Alison a sharp look.

'I have a second-year staff nurse coming from another ward with intensive care experience.' Alison considered the child on the bed, the awful stillness, and the pallor of the thin little face, and came to a decision.

'No . . . Staff Nurse Manning had better look after her. It will mean finding someone else to organise the ward, but I think it would be best.'

'Whatever you say.' Steve lifted a flaccid hand. It looked amazingly small inside his big fist, and Alison turned away feeling suddenly emotional. This would never do. She had the child's mother to see. Nursing staff in tears didn't inspire much confidence.

'I'll be in theatre for the next hour or so. Ring if you want me, I don't mind. I'd rather know if there are any changes.' Steve tucked a blanket around the child and walked to the door. Looking back he smiled at Alison. 'Chin up.'

'Mrs Cary?' Alison approached the slight, attractive-looking woman, waiting in the small room adjacent to the office. Mrs Cary stiffened, her eyes red-rimmed, frightened.

'Betty . . . Is she still unconscious?'

'At the moment . . .' Alison began gently.

'Doctor said it could be hours, days . . .?' Mrs Cary

wrung her hands, her face, still young, had the bloodless look that comes from perpetual weariness.

'Yes, I'm afraid we can't tell at this point.' Alison led the distraught woman to a chair and sat down beside her. 'You've come quite a long way—have you your own transport, Mrs Cary?'

'No.' Mrs Cary gave a hopeless shake of her head. 'There's only the two of us, Betty and me. The boys went with their dad when we split up. They got to take the milk to the station every morning and they need the ute. There's an old car on the farm Will was trying to fix up. Hasn't had much luck with it.' She was slightly hysterical, Alison held her hand and let her talk. When Mrs Cary was more in control of herself, she said quietly,

'Then it's possible for you to stay in town, perhaps.' Alison allowed the suggestion to sink in for a moment.

'Yes, I would want to do that so I can be near her.' Mrs Cary looked at Alison uncertainly. 'Would it be very expensive, do you know, Sister?' The work-worn hands were agitated and Alison noted the clean, carefully pressed shirt, threadbare at the elbows and fraying slightly at the cuffs, the neat cotton skirt and sensible inexpensive sandals.

'You could probably have a room in the Nurses' Home, if you wouldn't mind that.' Alison was sure it could be arranged somehow. The arrangement sounded perfectly feasible, she saw no reason why Mrs Cary couldn't be put up while her daughter was so ill when a number of the rooms were empty.

She left a very much relieved Mrs Cary with a fresh cup of tea and hurried back along the corridor, stopping in on the side rooms to run a critical eye over the observation charts. In both cases, the red lines fluctuated wildly, making it difficult to predict whether or not there was any real change in condition. At such times Alison relied on a sixth sense. Over the years it had never let her down and she prayed that it would not this time.

She had a word of encouragement for the nurses looking

after the new admissions in the ward. Two children had already gone to theatre to have their injuries attended to under general anaesthetic. However, the nurses had their hands full with the three remaining, all of whom were showing signs of the fractious behaviour commonly associated with concussion. The nurses were remarkably calm and well organised—none of them were more than halfway in their training—and seemed to have thought of the essentials. Nevertheless on principle Alison did her own check on the post-operative recovery equipment and saw that it was in readiness for the children when they arrived back from theatre. Then she coaxed one irritable little girl into letting her nurse take blood pressure readings.

Further down the ward she stopped by Rosa's bed. 'And how's my poppet?' she crooned, picking her up. 'All better now? Hmmm. I haven't got time to take you with me today, but Nurse will be along in a minute with your tea. You'll like that.' The thin little arms encompassing her neck held on tightly. Rosa knew what she wanted, and tea wasn't in sight yet. 'Mistake picking you up wasn't it?' Alison said softly, rocking the child in her arms. 'Ah—and what's this I see? It's your tea. Come on, I'll put you back.' Rosa opened her mouth to bawl and clung on tightly, but then she caught sight of the tray and the tempting portions on it and allowed Alison to hand her over.

'Thanks, Nurse,' Alison said with a grin. For a few brief minutes she watched Rosa being fed, and marvelled at the close shave with fate. The cut in Rosa's throat had closed over and was almost lost from sight in the baby ringlets; soon it would be only the faintest hairline to show where Alison had made the incision. In time, it wouldn't show at all. She hoped the other scars, the deeper ones of the soul, would heal as well.

The next two hours passed with a rush, and Alison was busy giving out the evening medication when Steve arrived back on the ward. 'You still here?' He was smiling, the lines in his face deeper after the long day, his blue eyes still worried. This evening he looked older than his twenty-seven years.

'Well, I see you are,' Alison said, looking up at him and smiling with him. They were both tired, but the pressure was off, the condition of the two seriously injured children having become less critical within the last sixty minutes. He told her what he had done in theatre and then walked back to the office and listened to the promise she had made to Mrs Cary.

'But then I ran into trouble,' Alison was saying, her brows drawn in a worried frown. 'Everybody said it was a great idea, but that it wasn't up to them, etc., etc. Both Matron and the Medical Superintendent are away—some conference or other—and nobody will commit themselves. They don't want the responsibility, or won't take it, of simply saying yes, go ahead.' She looked at him, still anxious but confident he would help, and was dismayed to see him shaking his head.

'It's precisely this reason I want the extra facilities, so people *can* stay overnight, but lord . . .' Steve ran stiff fingers through his hair, 'it was a bit rash, wasn't it, to promise her a room in the Nurses' Home. I'm sorry, Alison, I don't know what to suggest.'

Dismay turned to alarm. She had been relying on him. 'But—but you *know* people better than I do, I mean . . .' She refrained from adding that he was her best chance, seeing how he reputedly had all the woman in the place eating out of his hand.

'Mrs Cary doesn't live that far out in the sticks, does she? Couldn't she take a bus?' Steve looked at her hopefully. 'One leaves town after the movies get out, goes out to the Waimea Valley.'

Alison made a face, disappointed. 'She probably doesn't even have the bus fare on her.' She felt defeated, and because she was tired, she said crossly, 'Honestly, I thought you'd be more help.'

'You made the promise, you keep it,' Steve snapped. His face bore a strained expression. God, what a day! He had worked without a break for eight hours, not so much as a cup of coffee. He still had two sets of worried parents to see, and after that, a kid with a Colles' fracture to reduce. Which reminded him—he had a promise of his own to keep.

CHAPTER FIVE

'BUSY!' The voice cautious, apologetic almost, and vaguely familiar. Alison turned to find Trevor Smaille at the office door. 'I was visiting a friend so I thought I'd pop round and see if you were here. You're on late.'

'Ah . . .' Alison turned the key in the lock, made sure the drug cupboard was secure, then gave her attention back to the man at the door. 'Normally I'm not this late,' she told him with a courteous smile, 'but today has been anything but normal.'

'I heard about the accident.' He came into the office looking at her curiously. Was her veil crooked? Had she broken out in spots? wondered Alison. Perhaps he was appraising her uniform for future reference.

'Anything I can do?' His slightly bilious eyes dwelt earnestly on her face.

'I beg your pardon?' There was something very offputting about the man, and she couldn't think what.

'You see?' he brayed triumphantly, as if she had confirmed a deeply held suspicion. 'You medicos forget us lay people. We're predestined to languish in our offices uncalled upon.'

'Well, Mr Smaille, if I knew . . .'

'My dear girl, call me Trevor. I just wanted to let you know that we are here and always available in any emergency, and if there's anything we can do to help, you only have to ask. Anything, just say the word.'

'That's very kind of you, Mr Smaille,' Alison murmured politely. Presumably he was making this statement on behalf of the Board—and then it flashed through her mind. The Board. He was on the Hospital Board. He could help, indeed he could.

'Trevor,' he reminded her, his flat eyes still on her face, giving Alison an insistent feeling something was wrong with it. Maybe a tealeaf was obliterating her front tooth or something.

77

'Trevor,' she amended, smiling, but with lips firmly closed. Without wasting any more time she told him about the dangerously ill girl, whose mother wanted to stay somewhere close by. Trevor suggested the motel along the road which apparently always had vacancies. But Alison shook her head.

'No—you see, I don't think she can afford to do that. I offered her a room at the Nurses' Home, but I can't seem to make anyone realise how urgent this is. Nobody seems to have the authority to give me permission.' She smiled at him, and her smile seemed to suggest that if any person had authority, it was he, Trevor Smaille.

'Well . . .' He peered at her uncertainly, then seemed to fling caution to the four winds. 'I think it could be managed,' he said, beginning to exude self-importance. 'The Chairman is a good friend of mine. I'm sure we can fix something up.'

Alison was called away, and she left Trevor Smaille speaking in a deferential voice to someone on the phone, presumably the Chairman. When she came back, he was lounging in her chair, puffing at a cigar in complete disregard to her no smoking notice.

'All arranged,' he said, making no effort to move. But Alison was so pleased, she would have offered him the office and her chair for the night, if he wanted them. 'The Home Sister has been notified and you can rest assured there will be a room available for as long as your dear lady requires it, or until her daughter is off the critically ill list anyway,' he amended a little more cautiously.

'Oh, I can't thank you enough . . .'

'My dear,' he stood up and came over to stand so close to her Alison was obliged to edge back a step, 'I'm glad to have been able to assist. Now am I mistaken, or should you have been off duty hours ago?'

'Normally I would have been,' Alison's smile was uneasy. 'Actually, though, I was about to leave when you arrived . . .' She could have bitten out her tongue. Now he was about to insist on escorting her out of the hospital, and kind though he had been, she didn't want him to know she was without transport. She might yet be seeking a room herself at the Nurses Home—though she couldn't bear the thought of not having a change of clothing. The thing was, with her car in the garage again, she had relied on a lift home with Anne. Then because she had stayed on late, she had insisted Anne not wait for her—perhaps hoping Steve Barratt might offer a lift when he came to do his evening round. But he hadn't, and anyway, their parting had been none too cordial in the end.

Trevor also had been doing some thinking. 'You do have your car?' he raised his eyebrow, cocking his head a little to one side expectantly, as if he expected to flush her out. Alison reviewed several possibilities, but the fact remained, she did quite desperately want to get home to a hot bath, a change of clothing, and bed. Her own bed.

'I'm afraid I haven't, she conceded, after a long pause.

'Well,' he smiled moistly, 'then I'll run you home.'

Oh well, thought Alison, she was going to get home, and that was the main thing. And really, what did she have against the man? He had been kind, and very helpful, besides which, he was quite personable-looking. Not good-looking in the way Steve Barratt was—but then very few men were, and she had to remind herself how in the beginning she had held those extraordinary good looks against him. It was almost ironical to think that she now compared other men to him on that basis. Why she thought she had to compare them at all?

On the way home Alison made an effort to appear interested in what Trevor Smaille was discussing, but it was an uphill task. She was tired, and what with the rather monotonous tone of his voice and the deep leather cushioning, she found she had to fight to keep her eyes from closing.

With a start, she realised they had come to a stop. She struggled up in her seat. 'Where are we?'

'I think this is where you live.'

Alison looked blankly at the familiar high hedge outside her window. 'I went to sleep, didn't I?' she said stupidly. Turning to look at him, 'I'm terribly sorry, I didn't mean to be so rude.'

'Not at all,' he said, though she thought he sounded a mite hurt. 'You were tired, don't give it another thought.' The least she could do was invite him in.

She was opening the front door when Steve pulled his Land Rover in by the gate. Alison paused, waiting on tenterhooks for him to get out, her hand still on the knob. Then as Kirstin climbed from the front passenger seat, her heart skidded to a standstill.

'Hello. Wait for us.' Kirstin waved from the gate and came tripping up the path in a delectable cotton shift that fitted where it touched, brown bare arms gleaming in the lamplight. It wasn't difficult to see how happy she was. Alison couldn't bring herself to look past Kirstin's slender shoulder at the tall shadowy figure following.

'Who have we here?' Trevor was eyeing Kirstin appreciatively. Alison introduced them. Behind Kirstin Steve Barratt glowered. Any man that looked at her the way Trevor was looking at Kirstin—Steve Barratt wouldn't even notice, much less be jealous about. It was surprising how much the thought hurt.

'Let's go in, shall we?' Kirstin's bright smile encompassed them all. 'Oh, but you've time for just one drink, surely?' she said, as Steve stepped back, preparing to take his leave. She ran back down the steps and took his arm.

'Sorry, but I'm dead on my feet.' Steve smiled and leaned over, kissing her softly on the cheek. 'Another night.' He glanced up at Alison, ignored a joky aside from Trevor, and with a cursory farewell, departed. Kirstin went with him to the gate.

'Come on in, Trevor,' Alison said, turning away. What did it matter who Steve Barratt was interested in? It wasn't her, and she was silly to ever let herself think he could be. With Trevor settled comfortably on the sofa in the front room, she went through to the kitchen where Anne was sitting over a mug of cocoa wearing curlers and her old bath robe and half an inch of lanoline on her face.

'Who is it?' Anne hissed, fearful of being discovered

looking her worst but too comfortable to make a move unless it was strictly necessary.

'It's only Trevor Smaille. Do you know him? He gave me a lift, so I thought I'd better do the decent thing and ask him in for a bite of supper. Kirstin's out there too.'

'Smaille? Smaille? Oh yes, I remember, bigwig on the Hospital Board.' Anne tightened her robe at the neck and patted a few rollers back under a scarf and cast an uneasy glance at the door.

'It's all right,' Alison said, having to smile. 'I won't be inviting him through.' She began searching the cake tins. Dinner being eaten early in the evening, it was usual to produce a substantial supper of scones, cakes and the like—a custom she was slow in adjusting to.

Returning to the front room with a loaded tray, she found Kirstin and Trevor in animated conversation, which was just as well, because she didn't feel very much like talking. In fact she was relieved to have him thus occupied. Setting out the supper things on the coffee table, she enquired about milk and sugar.

'A little milk, thanks, and two sugars.' Trevor's smile took in the buttered scones, Anzac biscuits and walnut squares. 'Which one of you girls is the cook?' He looked coyly at Kirstin and Alison in turn.

'Anne,' Kirstin said, then went on to explain about the third member of the household while Trevor settled himself to the comfortable business of eating.

Alison let them talk and settled back in an armchair and sipped her tea. One of the cats came and curled up in her lap and she absently stroked its sleek fur.

It had been another hot oppressive day, but now there was a faint breeze lifting the curtains, bringing a welcome coolness. Pusscat, as she was known, rolled over on her back, purring loudly. Alison rubbed her ears. It worried her that she had begun to feel so emotional about Steve Barratt. Nothing could be worse for a professional relationship than that. Maybe, she thought, stroking the black stripes into the grey and back again, maybe she was a little bit in love with him.

Trevor was reluctantly getting to his feet and Alison slipped Pusscat from her lap and stood up. The two girls saw him to the door, Alison thanking him again for the lift and for his help, and they waved goodbye.

'Nice guy,' Kirstin said, locking up behind them and turning off the lights.

'Isn't he,' Alison agreed, and went on to tell her about how Trevor had turned up in the ward and his help in getting Mrs Cary a room. She shrugged. 'There, you can never tell. Steve didn't even want to know, and Trevor comes along and arranges everything, just like that.'

'Oh, come on, that's not being fair.' Kirstin, gathering up the cups, straightened to look at Alison. 'You can't expect Steve to pull rabbits out of a hat. You did rather dump the problem on him. After the day he'd had, he was pretty fed up.'

She might have known he would have told Kirstin all about it. His version. What about the day she'd had? Seven admissions to fit in with everything else, the worry and strain that had stemmed from it. 'Well,' her voice sounded unnaturally high, 'if Trevor hadn't offered me a lift out, I would have been stranded. Steve knew my car was in the garage.' She was close to tears and she sounded ridiculous, petulant, downright childish.

Kirstin almost did a double-take. Could this be the reserved, unflappable Alison talking? She picked up the tray. 'Come on through to the kitchen, I'm going to rinse these while you have a bath, but first there's something you ought to know.' Alison trailed after her into the empty kitchen, Anne having fled to the safety of her own room.

'Steve actually went back to the ward. He was going to offer Mrs Cary the use of his own house while her daughter was in hospital, and he wanted to give you a ride back as well. Only by that time, you'd gone.'

'Oh . . .' Alison picked up a teatowel. The truth was, she wished Kirstin hadn't told her. How much easier it was to be angry with Steve. How much safer. But how could she harden her heart against a man when he went and did a lovely thing like that? 'He really went back to the ward?'

'Yes.' Kirstin took the towel from her hands. 'He told me all about Mrs Cary when he came down to the department. He'd promised to give an anatomy lesson to my pregnant mums and I was a bit surprised when he turned up, I thought he'd be much too busy to spare the time.' She stacked the dishes neatly on the rack. 'Anyway, he even had me ringing round to see what I could do. When nothing turned up, he suggested his house. I thought it was really nice of him. Poor old dear, he looked so tired, I felt sorry for him. Things aren't working out with Clair either, apparently, though quite honestly I can't say I'm sorry about that.' She glanced at Alison and was suddenly remorseful.

'There I go again. Talk, talk, talk. I didn't get in the way, did I, this evening? Oh, what a fool I am—of course I did. I'm sorry, I never thought . . .'

'No, don't be silly, of course not. I'm glad if you and Steve . . .' Just for a second Alison faltered. 'It was nice he gave you a ride home, you must be tired making the journey on the motor scooter. . .'

Kirstin was looking at her very oddly.

'No, I didn't mean Steve. I was talking about Trevor. What I meant to say was that I hoped I didn't monopolise his attention all evening.'

Alison hastily retrieved the towel and began drying a cup, only too aware of the gleam of curiosity in Kirstin's blue eyes. She wished she could think of something convincing to say, something guileless, that would dampen it. What a fool, to have jumped to the wrong conclusion like that.

'Say hello to Sister, Poppy.' Alison glanced up as Steve Barratt walked into the office with a toddler in his arms. She had meant to give him a clinically detached smile—no more nonsense, whatever terrible power he had to throw her heart into an uproar she must ignore—hence the clinically detached smile. But how could she resist the child in his arms? She clasped her hands, her wariness giving way to unrestrained delight. Two dark eyes surveyed her through a tangle of curls. Apparently finding her wanting, the child went back to munching on a large bar of chocolate.

'Who's this, then?' asked Alison as Steve sat down on a chair opposite and settled Poppy on his knee, apparently unperturbed by the messy hands and the imminent ruination of his freshly laundered coat.

'Poppy, what do you say to Sister?' Steve coaxed. In response Poppy bestowed a disarming smile on Alison and offered up the nibbled bar—but only for a second. The size of it amazed Alison.

'She can't possibly be meant to eat the whole bar of chocolate in one sitting?' Alison said, wincing slightly. Steve gave Poppy a dubious look.

'Gran gave it to her, and I suspect it's more than my life is worth to take it away. Poppy'd scream blue murder. Gran's along visiting with Rangi, by the way,' he grinned. 'It's all right, you haven't got a horse in the play-yard today.'

'I should hope not,' she told him sternly, watching Poppy eat her way steadily through the bar with a kind of morbid fascination. 'So this must be Rangi's little sister?' She looked up at Steve, forgetting how dangerous a thing it was to meet his eyes. And goodness knows, she never meant to.

'She is,' he said. Alison rescued her eyes from his hold.

'And is it true that the first Maori child goes to the grandparents to be raised?' she asked steadily.

'Traditionally it's the custom. If you're interested, why not come with me to the Meeting House when I take a clinic?'

'Could I? I'd like to.' Interest sparkled in her eyes. Then the phone rang and she took it. Steve watched her jotting down some lab results, unhurried but efficient, exchanging a few pleasant words, then hanging up. He still had a load of work to attend to. He wondered if he was procrastinating in her office on purpose. Alison put down her pen and looked up at him. 'What were we saying?'

'I forget. I was going to ask what kind of perfume you're wearing—I like it.'

Alison was saved from answering by a knock on the door. She placed a hand over her blazing throat and called, 'Come in.' A Maori woman of much dignity made an appearance.

Poppy beamed and waved her fists.

'By corrie, she got you in a mess all right, Doctor.' The woman came forward to claim her grandchild.

'Serves me right for putting on a clean coat.' Steve grinned and handed Poppy over, then introduced Alison. She was given a shy nod, and then Poppy's grandmother retreated to the doorway.

'My boy not giving any trouble, eh?'

'Rangi is one of my best patients,' Alison said warmly. This was accepted in silence. Gran shared the Maori community's suspicion of hospital Sisters dressed head to toe in unblemished white.

'The veil doesn't help at all, you know that,' Steve said when they were alone again. He studied the three-cornered triangle of starched muslin covering Alison's head with an exasperated eye.

'Uniform regulations were laid down long before I arrived,' Alison said in mild protest, having been herself surprised by the outmoded form of headdress.

'It's got to go, you know. It really has,' he told her with surprising gentleness.

'Well,' she shrugged, feeling at a loss, and really, she couldn't think of a thing to say in their favour, 'perhaps it would be a good thing if we did stop wearing uniforms—if it makes us that much more approachable.' Steve laughed.

'Can I have that in writing?'

'Not yet,' she told him with a smile. 'I haven't quite made up my mind to dispense with them. I have to make sure we can maintain standards of hygiene . . .' And before he could launch himself into a new line of attack, she hurried on to thank him for offering Mrs Cary the use of his home.

'Well, I'm just glad your friend was able to get her a room more convenient than my place is.' He flattened his voice, giving it the hard twang most commonly associated with a New Zealand accent. Alison suspected he did it deliberately sometimes, just to annoy her. Normally she enjoyed listening to him speak for he had the deep melodious voice of a bass singer.

'He is not my friend. I hardly know the man,' she said,

rising to the bait. She flipped open the report book with a hastily assumed air of detachment. If he didn't have any work to do this morning, she did. 'About Emma Fairchild,' she said, all briskness.

'She can go home.' His voice was rich and lazy again.

'Good. She'll be pleased about that.' Alison pencilled a note in. 'About the two head injuries—both are fully conscious now and off the critical list, so I wondered if we might put them in the ward with the others.'

'All right with me. But I want them kept on hourly observation, and I'd like to see them first. Can you do a round with me?'

'Yes, of course.' Alison finished making notes, then closed the file and stood up, automatically twitching her veil straight. Steve wondered if she would give it up. He couldn't force the issue on uniforms.

'By the way,' he gave her one of his oblique looks that left her wondering, 'I saw Burt on the way in. Your car will be ready to pick up later today.'

Alison scooped cat food from a tin while Pusscat rubbed round her ankles. 'All right, all right, here you are.' She bent down and ran her hand up the curving back and placed the bowl on the floor. 'And you, Princess,' she called softly to the Siamese who had been watching the proceedings with slit-eyed disdain. The phone rang and she hurriedly placed down the second portion.

Her aunt's voice came anxiously over the line. 'Thank goodness you're there! Alison, Sue-Ann's been in an accident, she's been admitted to hospital.'

'Oh Aunty, no! Is she badly hurt?'

'No, thank God. But it's awful. The car she was in was stolen.' Alison listened to her aunt, horrified at what she was hearing. She gathered there had been an accident, with several youngsters involved. Going for a joy-ride, May said. May herself was confined to bed with a leg ulcer that had opened up, and Henry and the boys were up-country mustering sheep and wouldn't be home until the next day. It all sounded terrible. 'You must try and not worry, Aunty,

I'll go in and see Sue-Ann right away,' said Alison. 'But what about you? How are you managing, confined to bed?'

'Don't worry about me, love. Irini has been over and her boys are very good, and it's only for a few days, the doctor said. I just feel such a fool, not being able to drive, and being in this situation at a time like this. But if you would see Sue-Ann, it would be a weight off my mind. Give her my love.'

Alison didn't waste any time. She stopped by the kitchen to grab her sweater from a chair, for the evening had turned suddenly cool, and dashed out to the car. Lucky she had it back.

The hospital was still busy with visitors hurrying in before visiting hours ended. The porters had not yet collected the squat stainless steel kitchen trolleys and they sat outside the wards looking like monsters from another planet. Alison pushed open the doors of Women's Surgical, and very nearly collided with two policeman on their way out.

'Oh . . . Sorry.' She smiled and was about to pass on when she suddenly remembered May saying something about the police being involved. Both looked impossibly young and harmless, nevertheless their smart blue uniforms carried the full weight of authority and struck an ominous note.

'Anything the matter, Miss?' The taller one of the two was quick to run an appreciative eye over Alison's slender form, from her floating shiny hair to her bare sandalled feet. Alison smiled, shaking her head, and hastened on her way.

Stopping by the office door, she was told Sue-Ann's place in the ward by a harassed-looking staff nurse who took scant notice of the enquirer, and certainly didn't connect the girlish figure with the severely uniformed Sister seen at a distance in the hospital cafeteria. In reply to a few questions, Alison found out that Sue-Ann was comfortable, her injuries not extensive, and she wasn't expected to remain long in hospital. Leaving it at that, Alison made her way down the ward and stopped by a screened-off cubicle. A student hurrying out with a tray told her she could go on in.

Steve Barratt was lounging on the one chair, long legs stretched out. He glanced up in surprise at Alison and quickly got to his feet.

'What are you doing here?' she blurted to fill the silence.

He laughed, 'I might ask you the same.' They both turned and looked at the girl in bed. Sue-Ann managed a small embarrassed smile. Apart from a light graze down the side of her face and a bandaged wrist, there seemed little evidence of any other damage from where Alison stood.

'I've come to see Sue-Ann,' Alison said.

'You mean Suzie.' Steve bestowed the kind of smile on her one gave to people suffering an unfortunate lapse in memory.

'Huh-oh!' Sue-Ann slid further on down her pillows so that only her face and a quiff of lilac hair protruded from the top of the sheets. 'You two know each other?'

'You could say that, Suzie.' Steve turned a quizzical eye on her.

'Suzie?' Alison said, frowning slightly as she recalled the story Steve Barratt had told her about the incorrigible Suzie and her less than adequate adopted parents. Her eyes met his. 'I don't understand.'

Steve banged the sauce bottle down on the table. 'How was I to know Suzie's foster-parents were your sainted aunt and uncle? Though if your Henry is anything like his brother it could explain a lot.'

Alison cranked furiously at the black pepper pot and glared at him. They had repaired to the cafeteria in an effort to sort the matter out, and though their discussion had started amicably enough, it had since taken a turn for the worse.

'You can leave my father out of it,' she said in a voice low enough not to attract the attention of the other tables, and then ignoring her own counsel, she fumed, 'You wouldn't be half the doctor if it hadn't been for the training he gave you. The time and effort he lavished on you lot.'

'*Lavished*'. Steve speared his knife through a sausage and waved it under her nose. 'The only thing he lavished on us was criticism.' With an effort he calmed himself. What was it about this girl that nearly drove him to distraction?

'That's not what I heard,' she snapped, looking at her fried eggs as if she meant to hurl them at him.

'Mind pouring the tea?' Steve asked drily.

'Oh, certainly.' She smiled sweetly. 'I'll be mum, shall I?' Steve refrained from uttering an insult that was on the tip of his tongue, simply because, with her sparkling eyes turned an angry sea-green, she looked outrageously beautiful.

'I know my Aunty May and Uncle Henry,' Alison said, pouring the tea with an unsteady hand, 'and they're the kindest, the dearest . . .'

'You can't know them very well if they managed to keep Suzie's history such a deep secret,' Steve said nastily.

'How smug you are! I've always thought that.' Alison set the teapot down on the formica table with a clatter. He was right to a certain degree, though. The families had never been very close, it wasn't until she came out from England that she had got to know her aunt and uncle. She expected that May and Henry simply thought of Sue-Ann as their child and had never seen the point of discussing her history. Poor Aunty May, in bed with a leg ulcer, who was kindness itself, and Uncle Henry whom she had begun to rely on for his warmth and great good sense. She leaned forward and said through gritted teeth, 'You couldn't know what it's like to bring up children, foster or otherwise.'

'And I suppose you do.' Steve settled back to enjoy the sling. Oh yes, thought Alison, he thought she was just an old maid who had lost her first love and looked after other people's children. Always somebody else's. She straightened her shoulders and adopted an aloof expression. She'd twitch her veil if she had it on, decided Steve. He'd seen that expression before—to be precise, whenever the subject of changes in ward policy was brought up, and it meant, to all intents and purposes, the subject was closed.

'The trouble with you,' he said portentously, 'is you throw the baby out with the bath water. Meaning,' he said, leaning closer, 'meaning that you're never willing to compromise. It's either got to be one thing or the other, black or white. Well, life's not like that. Take for instance the question of whether the nursing staff will get rid of uniforms . . .'

'Oh, that again.' Alison glared at him. Of all the one-track minds! If he couldn't get what he wanted by rolling charm out like an Axminster carpet, he simply wore people down by his persistence. 'I thought we came to try and straighten out what was best for Sue-Ann,' she reminded him tartly. 'Car conversion, didn't you say?'

He searched her face for a minute, then sat back. 'Yeah, you're right. We're not doing her any good arguing.' He thought and said, 'I don't think they'll be able to pin anything on her because apparently she joined the others not knowing the car was stolen.' He shook his head. 'It could have been nasty, she was lucky not to have been thrown through the windscreen, she wasn't wearing her seat belt. Even so, she got a nasty shock and she'll have to be handled very carefully when she goes home. I wouldn't like to think your aunt and uncle will make it any rougher for her.'

'Rough on her? May's never been rough on anyone in her life and Uncle Henry spoils her like anything. It should be my aunt in hospital with her leg, not Sue-Ann.' Alison had some misgiving that Sue-Ann was not as innocent as she claimed. In a small farming community, you knew the kind of car your friends drove, and despite the possibility that the girl might have been taken in with a plausible explanation, Alison couldn't think that there would not have been some boasting about their success.

'They worried about her a great deal, and perhaps at times they were over-protective, but they're certainly not the insensitive, plodding people you take them for. Just the opposite.' She added softly, 'And besides, they're the only family I've got.' She turned her face away and fumbled in her pocket, and Steve realised that she looked about to cry.

'Alison . . .' She blew her nose and looked at him fiercely, daring him to mention it. Steve moved uneasily in his seat. 'Well, I'd like to meet them some time,' he said, but without relish. He began buttering a roll, thinking he had handled that well enough to calm her down. When she picked up her bag, he raised his face in alarm.

'Don't go.' The funny thing was, he wanted her to stay. He grinned. 'We can squeeze another cup out of the pot, can't we?' When she accepted it, with one of her grave little nods, he smiled expansively and said, 'Suzie . . . I can't seem to think of her as Sue-Ann . . . anyway, she liked the things you brought in for her. Were the flowers from your own garden?' Alison nodded. He waited for her to say something, and when she didn't, he glanced at his watch.

'I've got an appendix being lined up for me in theatre. Came in after you left this afternoon.' He caught her expression. 'I know this sounds like a replay, but if I gave my word not to ravish you until at least we have the job done this time, would you come and assist me?' He was smiling, but there was none of the soft teasing about it she hated so much.

'Well, what about it?' He touched her hand lying on the table, his fingertips gently tracing her fine bones. It was impossible to say no.

'Stuart Dalgleish is pleased he doesn't have to turn out for this one,' Steve told Alison. 'He's over in the quarters watching the Test Match on the box.' They stood side by side at the sink in the white-tiled scrub room adjacent to the main operating theatre. Steve rinsed his first lather and applied liquid soap to his elbows. 'We thought she might settle down, but her tum looked a bit distended when I went back an hour ago, so I arranged for her to be done. Don't want to risk peritonitis developing later in the night.' He reached for a sterile towel and one of the theatre nurses came to stand respectfully behind him waiting to tie the strings of his gown.

As Alison shrugged her way into her own gown, and found it went to her ankles, he glanced over. She could tell he was laughing by the way his eyes crinkled at the corners. Unperturbed, she carefully slid her hands into the powdered gloves lying open for her and using the technique taught her in London, snapped the ends over her gown sleeves and followed him through to the operating table.

The scrub nurse was preparing the patient's abdomen with surgical iodine.

'Evening, Mr. Barratt,' the nurse greeted him, and Alison was favoured with a curious glance. The anaesthetist was jotting down some calculations and he too looked up.

'Ah, it's the lass who did the tracheostomy. Welcome aboard, Sister. Ready when you are, Steve.' More curious glances from the nurses, then Alison was handed one end of a sterile drape, and from then on, it was as if she had never been away from the operating theatre; the familiar hushed preparations, the big glareless overhead lamp, and the scrub nurse with her endless supplies, the anaesthetic machine humming and gushing, the electronic monitors and intravenous equipment—it was all there, familiar, unforgettable.

Steve stood on the other side of the table ready to start. For an instant her eyes met his, a fraction of a second, but enough to know she was with him. He took up the knife and made an incision at McBurney's point. His cut was clean and swift, extending down into the fascia. He discarded the skin knife and they set about clamping the bleeders.

Some surgeons plunged in with all the finesse of an Irish wolfhound. But not Steve. Alison watched his gloved hands moving with an infinite patience and delicacy. He explained as he worked, a natural teacher, showing her how to unclip artery forceps with a quick one-handed movement—something that looked easy, but required fingers of tensile steel.

Alison held the muscles of the abdominal wall aside with retractors and was gratified to see him wait for his scrub nurse to count the swabs before incising the peritoneum to enter the cavity. Most surgeons required their instruments nurse to keep up and keep count on swabs as they went. At the end of the day it was the nurse's responsibility, not the surgeon's, if anything was left inside, and bad luck for the patient. And if a nurse couldn't keep up and keep count, it was shipout time. 'Get out of the kitchen if you can't stand the heat,' Alison had heard a surgeon snap at one instrument nurse who couldn't keep pace.

Steve was quick, but he was careful, and his exploration detailed and cautious. Lucky patient, thought Alison, already assessing the child's recovery rate on the basis of his skill and care. No wonder there were so few post-operative complications on the ward!

'Ah-hah! Look at this. Another few hours and the appendix would have burst.' He stood back and allowed Alison to examine the oedematous organ. Then with minute care, he secured a section of gangrenous tissue, pared it cleanly from the healthy section and placed it in the kidney dish reserved for contaminated objects.

Before closing the peritoneum he stopped while the count went on for swabs, sharps, and instruments, then proceeded again. The tension in the theatre relaxed as he made the closure in a series of swift steps, the anaesthetist wandering round to tell Alison one of the many jokes that had a habit of surfacing in the operating theatre. He had been itching to know how she fitted into the scheme of things. It wasn't usual for a Ward Sister to be invited down to assist. To observe, yes. The cool eyes over the top of the mask roused a challenge in him. He wanted to see more of her.

'How about your beautiful assistant joining us for a drink later?' he asked Steve.

'Sorry, she has to be up early tomorrow.' Steve glanced at the head of the table and the anaesthetist went back to the task of restoring their young patient to the world of consciousness.

Alison had been amazed by Steve's casual remark. Tomorrow was her day off and she had already decided to stop in at the hospital and visit Sue-Ann and then go on out to the farm to see May. She hadn't planned on an especially early start.

'How is your embroidery work?' Steve asked, glancing up with smiling eyes. Alison held out her gloved hand for the needle holder. She had become proficient at suturing working nights in a London hospital, when the house surgeons were scarce on the ground, and the consultants simply not available for minor things.

'I thought you might like to come with me tomorrow

morning,' he said quietly, watching her neat interrupted sutures with satisfaction. 'I have a clinic at the Maori Meeting House.'

Alison felt a keen disappointment. 'I should have liked to. I can't, I'm afraid.' She reached for the surgical spray and aimed at the row of sutures. The nurse was ready with a gauze strip. Then there wasn't time to talk any further until they had the patient transferred to a trolley and on the way to recovery.

Alison was tugging at the knot in the back of her gown in the scrub room when Steve came up behind her and jerked the strings free. After spending an hour cocooned within its heavy folds under the hot lights, she felt hot and sweaty, and it was a relief to peel it off. The regulation cotton dress she had on underneath clung damply and all too revealingly to her body. Steve leaned an elbow on the wall above her and looked down. Suddenly he was no longer the detached surgeon. He was all man. And he was too close—alarmingly close.

'Allow me.' He pulled the tight cap from her head, releasing her hair in a cloud about her shoulders. 'Is that better?' His hair was tousled, his blue eyes baiting her with good humour, he was laughing down at her. Was it any wonder women found him irresistible? Alison wondered, hot and flustered and nervously brushing a curtain of silk from her cheeks.

'Now tell me, what's so important you can't make it tomorrow?' His voice had an unfamiliar softness, and he was still far, far too close. She tried to explain about her Aunty May.

'Could be that Suzie will be allowed out by tomorrow afternoon and we'll be back by then. Why don't you pick her up and take her out to the farm and see your aunt? What do you say now?'

CHAPTER SIX

'THE GOSSIPS are bound to have a field day, but I shouldn't let that worry you.' Anne stood up from the table and drank the rest of her coffee at a gulp. She started earlier than Kirstin, and Kirstin had already left.

'I didn't say I was worried exactly . . .' Alison helped herself to a scoop of marmalade. 'It's a good idea for a hospital Sister to visit a rural clinic, I can't think why it hasn't been done before.' And then, frowning, 'Or has it?'

'You're really wondering if Steve's in the habit of luring nursing staff into the country for a day of debauchery. Now admit it.' Anne grinned impishly, not waiting for an answer. 'He takes his clinics too seriously for that. His private life?' She shrugged. 'Frankly I don't believe all the gossip that goes round. Clair Manning's behind half of it, I'm sure, and it's probably wishful thinking in her case.'

'Then you don't think anything much is going on between those two?' Alison asked, her voice casual.

'Not any longer far as I know. Believe me, she'd be insufferable if there was.' Anne scrabbled in her bag for her car keys while Alison propped her elbows on the table and sipped her coffee, eyes half closed.

'I rather think he's got a thing for Kirstin, though,' she murmured, watching Anne thoughtfully.

'If he has he hasn't done much about it, then.' Anne upended her bag on the table and was rifling though the contents. 'Kirstin's been falling over herself to catch him, lord knows, and who wouldn't. But all he's done so far is kiss her on the cheek.'

'Whose keys are those in the fruit bowl?' Alison asked. Anne groaned, and swept the pile of miscellaneous items back into her bag, then snatching up the bunch she made for the door.

'Why don't you ask him yourself?' she called back. 'You're

beginning to know him rather well, I'd say.'

'You can't help getting to know someone you work with every day,' Alison called after her. But Anne had apparently gone, and she added aloud, 'But that doesn't necessarily mean I can ask him how many women he's on intimate terms with.'

'I heard that,' Anne said, diving back into the room and grabbing a jacket she meant to drop at the cleaners, 'and I would, he'd probably be tickled to death to think you care.' Alison threw her a pitying smile and told her to go or she would be late, then sat too long over her coffee and was herself late in getting ready. She was rushing round in a mad panic when the Land Rover pulled up outside the gate.

'G'day, puss.' Steve Barratt crossed over the verandah and bent to rub the tabby's ears. He straightened up as Alison appeared at the front door, his blue eyes taking in her smart uniform. He himself wore jeans and a faded denim shirt.

'I thought . . . seeing it was a hospital visit,' mumbled Alison, feeling silly now in her stiff white hospital clothes. 'I'm not wearing my veil,' was all she could think of to add.

'I can see that,' Steve said in his slow, half amused voice.

Flushing, Alison said, 'If you think I ought to change?'

'Nope. Moana will be in her uniform—if you can call it that—but maybe the stockings and shoes, perhaps. May as well be comfortable.' Alison hesitated. 'I don't mind waiting,' he said. As if to prove the point he squatted down to balance on his heels, his arms on his knees, and wriggled a stalk of rye grass for Pusscat to pounce on.

When she came back, bare-legged and wearing sandals, he was half sitting on the verandah railing, his face in the sun, eyes half closed. 'Ready?' he asked, turning his head lazily. The immeasurable, ineffable blue of his eyes washed over her. 'You're getting a nice tan, you know that?'

When they were on the road he told her they were heading for the small township of Swampy Creek and gave her a sidelong grin. 'It's what we call a one-horse town. There's a main street, a few houses, general store, a couple of pubs, and the Meeting House where the Maori community get together.'

Alison asked about Moana, the nurse who ran his clinic. Steve answered when he had snatched an opportunity to pass a truckload of cattle on the narrow road. 'Moana? She's one of the great people of this world. You'll like her. To begin with she's the district nurse. OK, it's a small population, but her territory covers an awful lot of country, some of it pretty rough. She recently did a health survey on her area, and it's first rate.' Steve squinted into his rear vision mirror.

'Will you take a look at that? Bastard's driving a trailer the size of a house and he wants to make a race of it. There's a radar trap up ahead that'll slow him down.' As he predicted, they soon lost sight of the trailer and Steve continued telling her about Moana.

'Ever hear of the Maori Council? No? Well, it's an important body. They take the initiative for their own affairs and for improving the welfare of the Maori people. Moana is on that, she is also the Maori Woman's Welfare League representative, and that outfit covers the cultural, social and educational side of things. So you see, she does a lot more than weighing babies and looking down people's throats. In fact, she is integrated herself with all facets of community life, and that's a concept very dear to my heart.'

Alison was smiling. It was a concept that had been very dear to her father's heart and he had tried to inculcate the idea into his students, with a fair amount of success, evidently, but she dared not tell Steve that. But quite suddenly, she saw it was what he was trying to do at the hospital, only in a somewhat different guise. In Steve's case he was trying to bring the community into the hospital, but with the same end result in mind.

As she pondered, they turned inland on a road she was not familiar with and she found herself looking across burnt paddocks where only a few sheep were dotted here and there. It was still quite early in the day and already the sun hung hot and heavy in a faded blue sky, and away beyond the paddocks, the mountains were lost in shimmering blue haze.

'I met Mrs Cary's husband last night when I went back to see the appendix case,' Steve said, breaking a long companionable silence. 'He'd taken the missus out for a meal. Nice if they got back together again.' he glanced at Alison sitting demurely by his side, hair coiled in a neat loop on the crown of her shapely head. 'Their little girl came out of it well,' he continued, eyes reluctantly returning to the road. 'She had me a bit worried there for a while.'

'She had us all a bit worried,' Alison agreed with a smile. They had been climbing a dusty road cut into the side of a hill. At the brow, she glimpsed a small settlement in the valley below. After the ochre-coloured hills they had travelled through, the valley was surprisingly green, with big dark trees massed together and clumps of weeping willows following the line of a creek as it snaked its way past the wooden houses. Most houses were painted in bright colours and had washing hanging from a line, and nearly all boasted a neatly cultivated vegetable garden.

'This is it,' said Steve. 'Swampy Creek.'

'From the number of houses you can't be expecting many people,' Alison observed.

'Don't you believe it. People come from miles around, and if the word gets out I've got a pretty young hospital Sister along there'll be hordes . . . Crikey!' Steve braked sharply as they rounded a bend and came upon a flock of sheep on the road. A careful driver always on the defence, he was able to bring the Land Rover to a complete stop. Within minutes the sheep had fanned out and they were in the middle of a woolly mass. Behind came the sheepdogs, tongues lolling, and a big sleepy-looking horse with the drover slouched in the saddle. As the sheep pattered sedately past, the dogs paused to inspect the tyres.

'Nice morning,' Steve said, leaning companionably out the window as the rider came abreast.

'Too dry,' the man said, tipping his wide-brimmed hat back on his head to squint at the sky. 'Rain's what we need.' He settled back in his saddle and seeing Alison, tipped his hat again. 'G'day, miss.' The horse gave a resigned heave, and they passed on.

Steve grinned. 'Typical farmer,' he muttered, moving off again, 'He'll be complaining about flooding the moment it looks like rain.'

'Kettle's on . . .' Moana was a slim dark-haired woman in her early forties with a lively smile. She emerged from the back room clutching a bunch of flowers in one hand and a vase in the other. Steve took Alison by the arm and led her forward to be introduced.

'I hadn't expected anything quite so beautiful,' Alison said, gazing around the long high-roofed hall with its handsome pillars of carved kauri wood and decorated wall panelling. 'I've seen carving like this only in the British Museum,' she gave a small astonished laugh. 'I thought it was a fairly new building?'

'It is,' Moana said, pride in her voice. 'All the wood carving was done by young Maori men during their three-year apprenticeship at the Rotorua Institute for Maori Arts and Crafts. The ancestral arts almost died out, so now the old are teaching the young their skills.' She showed Alison baskets and mats woven from the traditional flax plants, and the taniko weaving used in the making of decorative bodices and headbands. 'We hold classes for just about everything to do with the Maori culture—even a kindergarten for children where the Maori elders teach them Maori, in an effort to keep the language going. *Te koohanga reo*. It means the language nest'.

As they walked round, Alison paused to look at an oil painting of a beautiful young girl with a huia feather in her raven black hair and a greenstone ornament on her throat. An ancestral cloak lay round her shoulders and in the background were the shadowy figures of three old Maori women. There were other paintings, some of Maori chieftains, proud warlike men with full facial tattoos.

'You must come back when we have a special Maori feast and enjoy some of our local foods cooked in nature's way in the earth oven, or *hangi*, as we call it in Maori.' Moana smiled. 'But for now, Sister Prentice, I can only offer tea and sandwiches.'

'Call me Alison, please do,' said Alison, taking a tremendous liking for this remarkable, unpretentious woman, who combined so much in her life.

Alison was ushered into a large room at the rear end of the hall, furnished simply with a large wooded table, basketweave chairs and many cupboards. There was a sink for washing up and some kitchen equipment and whatever space was available on the walls was covered with paintings done by the very small children, with their name and age printed in big round letters at the bottom. Moana arranged her posy of Sweet Williams and placed the vase on the table. Steve, who had gone back to the car, reappeared carrying a cake-tin which he gave to Moana.

'Kata made some of her cheese and parsley scones.' On catching Alison's look of undisguised curiosity, he gave Moana a broad wink. 'I haven't told her about Kata yet, she thinks I have too many girlfriends as it is, don't you, Alison?' he teased.

'I really hadn't given it much thought,' Alison said, annoyed to have him think she was even interested, much less cared—and at the same time discomfited, remembering her breakfast-time conversation with Anne.

Moana was smiling as she set out the morning tea. She motioned for them to sit down. 'Mrs Te Renga will be in with her twins this morning,' she told Steve. 'And old Nana will probably come. She's overweight and has a heart, and Steve is the only *pakeha* doctor she'll come to, Alison. She won't go near a hospital and she makes her own medicine from plants. But she likes to hear what Steve has to say, all the same. Then she goes away and takes her Maori medicine.' Steve crossed one long leg over the other, listening, and every now and then he asked a question about this child or that. It was very peaceful, and then pandemonium broke out in the hall with the arrival of three mothers, each with a babe in arms and seven pre-school between them.

'Looks like we're in for a busy morning,' Moana observed

mildly. As more women began arriving the hall was taken over by the children, who ran out of control, chasing and shouting. The noise was deafening, and Alison wondered how a clinic could take place in the midst of these fearfully noisy youngsters. True, Moana and Steve seemed oblivious to the roars and manoeuvred between the eddying tide of children to talk to the adults. But then the mothers began marshalling the little ones into groups and handing out small parcels, which the children unwrapped and Alison saw contained crisp fried fritters and golden corn on the cob. The children were quite happy to be settled on the mats where they began to eat their picnic lunches, and a score or more brown eyes turned on Alison to watch her every move.

Peace and quiet having been established, the mothers took it in turn to talk to Steve, while the babies were examined and weighed by Moana and Alison, who then marked down the weight increase on the percentile charts. After the babies, they began on the two- and three-year-olds, and then it was the four-year-olds' turn.

'Tiny . . .' Moana smiled down at a brown wisp of a child. 'Why aren't you at school today?' Tiny stood with his doleful eyes upturned. An old Maori woman shuffled forward, her bare feet slapping the wood floor.

'They say he too little for school,' she claimed indignantly. 'They say he not five, eh.'

'But we know you're five, don't we, Tiny?' Steve said, dropping down to the small size and balancing on the balls of his feet.

'Mitt Willmott say I'm not,' Tiny said, sniffing, his eyes open very wide.

'Do you have his birth certificate, Mrs Wharepatea?' Moana asked, and old Nana shook her head.

'I can write my name and Nana say I can read like anything,' Tiny said, nodding, quite relishing all this attention.

After a hurried consultation with Steve, Moana said, 'Nana, I'll get a copy of Tiny's birth certificate from the Records Office, then you can show it to the headmaster, and I'll have a little word with Tiny's teacher, Miss Willmott, and Tiny will be able to go back to school.' Nana gave a dignified nod and Tiny went gleefully back to sit on the mat and be stared at in awe by the other children not old enough to go to school.

'He's so little,' Steve said softly to Alison. She swallowed a lump. The touch of compassion in this man could reduce her to rubble. 'You can't really blame the head for thinking he'd been slipped in ahead of schedule.' Alison nodded, watching Tiny counting up to ten on his fingers for the benefit of those not fortunate enough to be learning such things.

It seemed far too soon, when Moana looked around and said that was about it. 'I can't thank you enough for your help,' she said to Alison, as she escorted them both out to the Land Rover, the children crowding eagerly behind. The women too had come out on to the porch and they stood, laughing and waving. Some had been practising a *poi* dance, and they clicked their *poi-poi* in unison and broke into a song of farewell.

Alison was stirred by their warmth and spontaneity, and once again she felt the promise of tears in her throat and had to blink rapidly and hope that Steve was too busy negotiating his way round the parked cars and a few inconveniently sited cabbage trees to notice how emotional she had become.

'Feel like a dip?' Steve asked, when they were on the road once more. 'I've got a couple of towels in the back and I never go anywhere without my togs.' His tempting suggestion served to remind Alison how hot and sticky she was—and how green and cool the water had looked beneath the bridge. She stared at the strong brown hands gripping the steering wheel, studying them for a moment, as though she had only just discovered them. Of course she couldn't go for a swim, what was she thinking of? She didn't have her bathing suit.

'Never mind. We can get you one at the store, I told you they have everything.' Steve drew in by a low-verandahed shop sitting rather grandly on a street that had few such.

Inside the store, a woman with tumbled hair was wielding a can of fly spray and the frantic buzzing of dozens of dying flies could be heard. It was stifling hot.

'That's got the beggars. Now, what can I do for you?' She stood back behind the counter and looked at them expectantly. Alison, almost overcome by the close heat and the suffocating stench of fly spray, was gazing at the crowded shelves, and the salami and half-hams and strings of onions dangling from the ceiling, along with bill tins and pairs of boots tethered together with leather laces, and canvas packs; Steve was right, the store did indeed sell just about anything. Though when a suitable suit was eventually unearthed, Alison found it didn't do to be fussy about minor details like colour and style. Nevertheless they were soon on their way to the bridge, Alison's new purchase on her knee.

'You can take the manuka bushes, if you want,' Steve said with a grin, as they surveyed the stopbank for shelter. The clump of manuka afforded better cover that the willows, so Alison accepted with alacrity. He gave her a towel and wound his around his neck and they both set off.

Steve was rolling lazily on to his back when she slid into the silky green water and he laughed at her gasping at its surprising coldness. 'This isn't one of the thermal areas where the water is warm,' he told her. 'This creek comes from the cold Pininga stream.'

'Now you're telling me!' Alison said, between gasps. She turned on her back, letting the water flow luxuriously around her and floated, face upturned to the hazy sky.

'The kids use the bridge as a jumping off point,' Steve said, bobbing up at her side. He stared at her face in the shadowed green light, wanting to touch her.

'I'm glad they're still in school,' she laughed, then, disturbed by his nearness, 'Race you to the other side and back!' She turned in a flash and started off with a graceful over-arm stroke, her hair spreading in the water like a cobweb, arms glistening with brilliant drops, long slender legs no more than a faint pulsing under the water.

Steve watched her go, his professional eye registering the

anatomical detail and co-ordination of her body, frowning, because he had known the warm and urgent and desirable feel of that body, and the raging fever she'd set off in him in that one blind impulsive moment when he had kissed her. God knows, the nights he had lain awake thinking about it. He had tried to put the thing out of his mind, but it was still there—the excitement that smooth resilient flesh caused him, the passive way her shoulders drooped at times when she looked up at him with those grave eyes.

What on earth was going on with him? She'd made it abundantly clear she didn't want anything other than a professional relationship, Besides, she had that prat Smaille dancing attendance on her and she was obviously interested in him. Damn it, he thought irritably, Smaille was more her age anyway. Moodily he began swimming back to the stopbank.

Alison was at the bridge. She turned, treading water and brushing hair from her eyes. 'Spoilsport,' she cried, eyes alight with fun.

'Afraid I've got to be,' Steve called back over a muscular shoulder. 'Time's getting on.' He pulled himself up on the grassy bank, picked up his towel and walked along to the willow trees to get changed without so much as a backward glance. Alison watched, bewildered and more than a little hurt. Had she bored him so much? She couldn't hope to be as enchanting company as Clair and Kirstin would be, and obviously were. But it saddened her nevertheless. She felt dull and unattractive in the shapeless all-covering suit; it must have been sitting on the shelf since the second world war. And who was Kata anyway? Flaring up with wounded pride, she wondered where he found the time to be so dedicated to his work, with so many women demanding his attention. On the way home, however, driving rapidly through the shimmering afternoon countryside, she confined her questions to purely professional topics. And she was determined not to waste any more time and emotion thinking about him in any other capacity.

*   *   *

Sue-Ann looked up as Alison arrived. 'Good, now I can get out of here.' She hopped off her bed and stuffed the lurid magazine she had been flicking through into her duffle bag.

'Sue-Ann, give Alison a chance, she may not be ready to leave straight away,' Aunty May remonstrated weakly from a chair. She looked tired and ill, and Alison noted it with instant concern.

'Aunty, what are you doing here? You shouldn't be on your feet, you know what the doctor said.' She hurried forward to give her Aunt a hug and a kiss. 'And one for you too, Sue-Ann.'

'Oh, my leg's much much better, thanks. Henry brought me in, and I was wondering if you could take us back, though. He's gone to a ram sale and won't be back till this evening.'

'Mum . . .' Sue-Ann frowned with impatience, 'she would have anyway. That's why she didn't go out home this morning.' Turning to Alison and brightening, she asked, 'Can I see Steve before we go?'

'Dr Barratt, dear,' May corrected with a hopeless glance in Alison's direction.

'Well, it's not Doctor either, he's a Mister, isn't he, Alison?' Suddenly the petulance faded and Sue-Ann was pouting prettily. Alison swung round as Steve stopped at the end of the bed and surveyed Sue-Ann with a tolerant grin. 'You said you'd come and see me this morning,' she accused.

'Sorry, young lady. Forgot it was my Swampy Creek morning.'

'And I bet you went for a swim at the bridge,' interjected Sue-Ann, dimpling up at him. Alison belatedly realised that her own hair was wringing wet in its tight coil and she didn't want Sue-Ann putting two and two together, but fortunately her young niece's attention was much too taken up with Steve to spare Alison a second glance.

'Sue-Ann, you mustn't be so inquisitive,' May chided from her chair. She smiled at Steve, recognising him as the junior houseman she had seen years ago in the hospital.

'I'm sorry,' Alison turned apologetically and introduced

Steve to her aunt. His voice was polite and cordial and he held out a businesslike hand, and only Alison was aware of the careful scutiny—for how could May possibly know that behind that lazy sleepy-eyed look were the eyes of an inquisitor?

'If Sue-Ann is ready, perhaps we should be going,' she said nervously, thinking that he might be about to drop one of his needling little remarks that might worry the life out of her aunt after she had peeled away the charm with which it had been delivered. But May was blossoming under his smile, as every woman did.

'You must come out to the farm for tea one day,' she was saying. 'Alison will bring you.' A remark that had Alison groaning inwardly as she imagined what Steve would have to say to her uncle Henry.

'Yes. One day, perhaps,' she murmured, helping her aunt up from the chair and hoping Steve would take the hint and go. But Sue-Ann, who had a crush on the good-looking doctor, wasn't about to pass up a chance.

'Mum, why don't we ask him for tomorrow? I can do everything—the baking and all that sort of thing. Oh, go on,' she implored. And of course May had to say yes then, and of course Steve agreed. Probably only so he could criticise the way they were bringing Sue-Ann up, worried Alison. He was bound to upset them.

'We'd stopped thinking about Sue-Ann as a foster-daughter.' Alison was sitting with her aunt on the verandah watching the sky turn blood red in the half hour before darkness fell. For there was no twilight in New Zealand's semi-tropical north, only a curious stillness and peace, as though the day had been suspended, a feeling that was even more pronounced on the farm when the animals had been fed and settled for the night and the last chores attended to.

'I should have told you, I know.' May gave a pensive sigh. 'The liberal ideas I started off with—they worked out just fine with the boys. But Sue-Ann? Alison, that girl has sex built into her genes. She just knows what her body is for. Henry thinks that given the right environment and love, it will all work out. But I don't know, Alison. I think we've been too soft on her.' May leaned over and laid a workworn hand on Alison's arm. 'Don't get me wrong, I love Sue-Ann and I want to do the best for her. But I am worried.' And then she told Alison the whole distressing story.

Sue-Ann had been staying overnight at a friend's house. May had never liked the family, but she believed the children must choose their own friends, and Sue-Ann was an intelligent, bright child who knew her own mind. She hadn't then, been seriously concerned about her. Sue-Ann had survived those first traumatic years, she would survive adolescence. May didn't see herself a keeper of morals. She could only guide and advise and trust to her children's innate sense of right and wrong. Alison thought that Steve would find it hard to disagree with those principles.

'I was in town that Friday night doing my shopping,' May continued, 'and I saw Sue-Ann in a beat-up old car with about four or five others.' She glanced at Alison. 'I don't know if you've been down town on a Friday night just after closing, but all the young people of a certain type congregate in the milk bars and take-aways. Then they ride around the streets in these old heaps with the boys sticking their bare bottoms out of the windows.'

'And you saw Sue-Ann in one of these cars?' Alison asked quietly.

'Yes,' May said wearily. 'Piles of make-up, green hair, a regular punk look. Alison, she's only fourteen!' May's voice was filled with anguish, and Alison's heart went out to her.

'I called the house she was staying at. No one answered. I found out later the parents were at a party. Henry was away that weekend at a conference, so I had to get one of the twins to drive me over. We waited until Sue-Ann got back and then I insisted she come home with us. She didn't like it, I can tell you. But when I threatened to tell Henry, she calmed down and agreed. That was my mistake, of course. I should have told Henry everything. But I didn't. I promised Sue-Ann I wouldn't if she would stop seeing the crowd she had been running round with. Sue-Ann really loves Henry and she agreed.'

'Who was she with when she had the accident?' Alison asked.

'The same gang. The police are satisfied she had nothing to do with the car conversion, but the others will be going up before the court. But oh, Alison, she can be such a nice girl when she wants, a perfect sweetie. I'm terrified the next time she won't be so lucky. And that's why I want Henry to put his foot down and be really strict with her. No more freedom until she can learn to handle it. For her own sake, we must insist on it, because if we don't, the State will.'

Alison stared out into the gathering darkness. 'I've always thought children feel more secure when limits are set on their behaviour.'

'I'm sure you're right—I know you are. I'm Sue-Ann's mother in every real sense of the word, and yet I've failed her by not imposing the limits I might have if she had been my own child. She never really accepted me and I suppose I felt I would lose what little affection she had for me. I've never been as important to her as Henry, or the boys,' May said candidly and a little sadly. 'I'm just Mum, rather dull and a bit inclined to nag and make a fuss. But we'll see. I keep hoping.'

And then the men were home, bringing with them an aura of excitement from the outside world, Henry's voice ringing up the stairs wanting to know where his little girl was; the twins teasing, and each jostling to outdo the other; and Sue-Ann, face flushed and eyes sparkling, the centre of attention and giving a highly exaggerated account of the accident; and May serving dinner and smiling at them contentedly. It was a noisy, happy dinner table. They might have their problems, but they were a family, and Alison was suddenly envious.

After the twins and Sue-Ann had gone upstairs, Henry got out the heavy crystal tumblers and half filled them with brandy, and the three of them sat round the fire—for the evening had turned cool with an early frost—Henry looking at his papers and May knitting, the cat keeping a watchful eye on the two sheepdogs who lay just outside the pool of firelight. The brandy burned and her thoughts became soft and intimate, sliding and interchanging in their own order, the things she had thought important being relegated to the scrap heap as she remembered the look in the wonderful blue eyes as she came bare-legged on to the verandah in the morning sunlight. Images of a day that had been full of curiosity and delight jostled for attention and voices whispered. He was coming—he would be here at the farm the next day. Relaxed and sleepy, the tension gone, Alison wondered what kind of fantasy she could be dreaming about. Just because Steve had given her an appraising glance or two, had flirted with her occasionally—as he did with every woman—there was no need to run away with the idea that his visit to the farm had anything to do with his concern for her. He was coming to please Sue-Ann, and because he was interested in her welfare.

CHAPTER SEVEN

'TABLE'S all set. OK if I go now?' Alison stopped beating the cream and blew a strand of hair from her eyes. Sue-Ann wanted to be at the farm gate to welcome Steve when he arrived and she hopped impatiently from foot to foot.

'All right. If you've done everything your mum said . . .' They had insisted May go for a rest after lunch. Alison pulled the neck of her blouse open. It was hot, her clothes were sticking to her, even the curtains hung limp at the open windows in the heavy sulphurous air. In the distance she could hear the crash of thunder. With a sigh, she went back to beating the cream.

At a tap on the door behind her, she stopped, and looked around. Without warning he was there, his blue eyes striking her like a bolt of lightning. She felt her hand go to her throat as fire took possession of her body; she was trembling, as if her lover had come.

'The front door was open and no one was around, so I came on through.' The rich, pleasant voice held her captive. Steve's gaze slid down into the unbuttoned neckline of her blouse.

Hurriedly and furiously she snatched off her apron and tried to do something with the buttons, but nothing seemed to connect, and her blouse remained firmly undone, and as before, his gaze was on the deep V of her neckline. 'Goodness!' her voice came out several octaves higher than usual. 'You must have missed Sue-Ann by seconds. She went out the back door, and through the orchard. She wanted to meet you at the gate.'

'You should have woken me, Alison.' Her aunt appeared in pearls and a floral silk creation, nervously patting at her curls. Steve smiled, and bent his tall form slightly to her diminutive size.

'What a beautiful garden you have, Mrs Prentice.' May

110

gazed at him in delight. He had picked the one subject she was really interested in, and could speak with ease about, and she led him off to show him her treasures at once. Alison finished spreading cream and by the time she too had joined them in the garden, Sue-Ann was back and was casting agonised glances at her mother's dress, which would not have disgraced Royal Ascot.

'Come in, come in,' May said, fussing over Steve. She led the way through to the front room which housed her collection of antique furniture and was reserved for very special occasions. The tea was spread on a gleaming rosewood table and shrouded by pink voile as a protection against any fly that might have survived the holocaust of insecticide.

Steve folded his long body into a dainty chair and accepted a cup, saucer and plate, balancing them adroitly on his knee as if he was in the practice of taking tea every afternoon, and proceeded to hold forth about the vagaries of sandy soil and which plants grew best in what, and why, while Alison listened in growing astonishment. Was there no limit to the man's list of achievements? She had never seen her aunt open up to anyone liked this. Whenever her aunt paused to draw breath, he slipped in a well-placed question that sent her off again, not only about gardening, but about any number of other topics. How easy it was for him! Suddenly and mysteriously she found the thought unutterably depressing.

'Alison has a lovely garden at her place. Have you seen it, May?' His narrow quizzical look took in Alison. She had been very quiet. She disclaimed any responsibility for the way their garden looked, saying that if she helped with the weeding she was apt to pull out the flowers.

'I'm just sorry Henry and the boys can't be here. They're up in the top paddock fencing a slip. The soil erosion is bad in this area. We've tried all kinds of ground cover to hold the soil, but it seems the most successful is also poisonous to the stock.' May sighed and fingered her pearls pensively. 'But Dr Barratt, please have some of my special cake.' She cut a huge slice and handed it over, waiting tentatively for his approval.

'Delicious,' Steve mumbled, mouth full. 'You must give me the recipe so I can take it home to Kata.' Alison said nothing, telling herself she didn't even want to know who Kata was. She did hitch down the hem of her skirt a fraction, though. She couldn't imagine how anybody who looked as though they might drift off to sleep any minute could make her feel so undressed.

'Kata keeps house for me,' Steve explained, in answer to Sue-Ann who didn't have Alison's reservations about asking questions, and went on to explain that his parents lived not more than an hour's drive from Fort William. Alison turned the pieces of information over in her mind to examine intently, much as one might unusual shells discovered on the beach. At that point the phone rang and Sue-Ann shot off to answer it. She was back in a second, her face alight.

'Mum, it's Paddy. The McCullys are going eeling. Can I go? Paddy says we'll be back by ten at the latest. Oh, please, Mum!' Gone was the rather painful act at being grown up, in its place was a natural bright-eyed young girl who was slightly bored with all this talk about gardens and recipes and such, and was eager to be off doing more interesting things.

'You catch eels in the dark by torchlight,' May explained to Alison, after she had given her permission, and Sue-Ann had dashed off. 'It's tremendous fun, I sometimes go myself.'

'Certainly a lovely evening for it,' Steve observed, glancing idly out of the window, his eyes returning to Alison who was picking at her slice of cake as if food was the last thing on her mind. May's lips twitched.

'Why don't you take the doctor down to the pond at Soggy Bottom and show him where the kingfisher nests? I'll clear these away.'

'You'll do no such thing.' Steve was on his feet and taking the cup from her hand. 'We'll do that while you take a rest on one of those comfortable-looking chairs I saw on the porch.' It was the pièce de résistance. May was enslaved and she gave up any pretence of being anything but. She sighed happily.

'How kind and thoughtful,' she murmured. 'Well, if you insist . . . One thing we do have is a dishwasher, I'm thankful to say. While you're away for your walk I'll write out that receipe.'

While Steve carried the loaded tray to the kitchen, Alison cleared the debris away. She was ashamed now to think he would come and upset her aunt. His questions had been gentle enough not to wound and he had been unpresuming enough to leave the field quite open for her. And of course May had been delighted to have him listen. All that listening, thought Alison. He had managed to find out an awful lot about the family in the course of a couple of hours. She couldn't think it was only just technique. He had seemed genuinely interested. What kind of opinion had he formed about them? It was suddenly very important for her to know, for she guessed he would have worked out some careful answers.

'If you don't really feel like the walk—it's quite a long way, you know—Aunty won't mind if you slipped away.' Alison wanted to give him the opportunity to leave, if he wanted to take it.

'I wouldn't miss the chance of seeing a kingfisher for anything,' Steve assured her. He twiddled expertly with the knobs and settings of the dishwasher and then pronounced himself ready when the machine started an efficient humming.

Alison led him through the gate and they started off along the rutted dray track that skirted the home paddock and led to the lower pasture, ignominiously known as Soggy Bottom. For a time they walked in silence, and then they both started talking at once. 'No, you first,' Alison said, blushing. A sudden breeze threatened to lift her skirt, and she clutched at it, distracted.

'Your aunt is a very nice lady,' Steve said thoughtfully, 'and I wouldn't want to say anything to her that would worry her unnecessarily.'

'About Sue-Ann?' Alison asked quickly.

'Yes. I've been doing some checking up, and it would appear that Sue-Ann has involved herself with a pretty rough crowd. Tell me what you know of the situation?' Alison looked up at the big man by her side and a tide of faith in him loosened her tongue for the first time that afternoon and she talked until she was out of breath, telling him all she knew.

'I think,' he said at length, 'someone had better have a good talk to her before she gets herself into real trouble.' He looked down at Alison. 'I was hoping to meet your uncle Henry.'

'Sue-Ann thinks a lot of him and maybe she'd take notice. I do know she'd listen to you, though. Perhaps you could have a talk with her some time.'

Steve was laughing. 'You're going to make me eat my words! Yes, well, I'll give it a try. I can't promise anything,' he said, touching her arm.

They left the track and started off through the long dry grass. A wind had started up, bringing the sound of the distant surf and whirls of dust and leaves, and flattening their light cotton clothing to their bodies. A goldfinch flew overhead, buffeted by the wind. The pond where the kingfisher had made its home was spring-fed and always full. Alison led the way to it through the flax bushes and reeds.

'There . . .' She pointed at a black beech. 'He sits on that branch up there in the sun. But I don't see him. In this wind, though, I'm not surprised.' She walked on to the edge of the pool and sat down on her heels, locking her arms tightly about her knees. She heard Steve's tread in the grass behind her.

'There's something I wanted to ask you.' Steve watched the bowed head. When she didn't move or turn round, he cleared his throat. 'Gilbert Hains has decided to take an early retirement and he's throwing a shindig . . .' Steve cleared his throat again, wondering why the heck this was so difficult all of a sudden. 'I'd like to take you along. If I may,' he added, beginning to feel downright nervous. Alison turned her head, looking up at him, as if he had said something extraordinary.

'You're asking me?' Alison had heard the others talking about the party as if it were the social event of the year. She was scarcely thinking, only marvelling that he was asking her, and yet not quite believing it. Then as he nodded, his blue eyes smiling into her own, she knew it was true.

'I'd love to,' she said in a half whisper, her heart beating crazily in her breast. And then came the first loud crack of thunder as the sky closed in where only minutes before the goldinch had flown, and fat drops of rain began splashing on her nose.

'We're going to get wet. Come on.' Laughing, Steve caught her hand, pulling her up. And suddenly she was in his arms, her warm, vibrant body responsive, her breath sucked out of her. He locked her tightly against him and took possession of her mouth, meeting her tongue with jet-like thrusts, the blood pounding in his veins.

Alison's half moan, half sigh, was lost in the wild keening of the wind in the trees. As the storm crashed over them, he pulled her head into the shelter of his shoulder and she stood clinging to him, the rain running down her face, her hair in straggling wisps, her blouse transparent in the wet. He said hoarsely, 'We'd better make a run for it. I wouldn't want you to catch your death.' For if he didn't this minute restore her to her family, he would find himself making love to her, by the reeds and rushes in the drenching rain.

Later on, when he had departed with the remains of the fruit cake, and several recipes, Alison turned a flushed face to her aunt. 'He asked me to a party. Me!' She shook her head. 'I still can hardly believe it.' Her gaze returned to the spot she had last seen the Land Rover. 'Oh, Aunty, to think that he asked me! Isn't that the most wonderful thing?'

May was looking quite perplexed, and Alison smiled. Her aunt most probably thought she was accustomed to having handsome young men invite her out to parties. The truth was, ever since James, there had been no man with the power to disturb her. She had sunk deeper and deeper into her solitary state, refusing invitations at first, and then not even seeking the companionship of another man. And then

Steve, and her unexplainable feelings about him.

She was still staring out the window, seeing nothing, just enjoying feeling happy. It was a precarious happiness. She couldn't expect Steve to feel the same way. But at that moment she simply didn't care. She was falling in love with him and it was wonderful. This marvellous man had come into her life and swept her off her feet. And if he had done it to so many others before her, who was she to complain? Oh, there were plenty of little voices, warning. But she was going to ignore them all. Later on, she knew, there would have to be an accounting, but not now. Not now when she was so happy. Later. When she could be more sensible about him.

'Rangi King was discharged yesterday,' Chris Laidlaw was telling Alison the next morning during report. The night nurse waited for Alison's face to lose its soft smile, knowing how keen she had been for the boy to stay longer in hospital, or at the very least, be sent to a children's health camp to convalesce until he was strong enough to go home to the austere life the family lived on the Island. But the soft dreamy expression remained and Chris wondered if she had taken anything in at all.

'Rangi King,' Chris repeated. 'His dad picked him up and took him home. Mr Barratt discharged him.' There, that would get a rise out of her.

'Not on horseback, I hope,' Alison murmured, and vaguely looked through the day's operating list, adding mildly, 'I don't want the child back with another bout of pneumonia.' Chris began to wonder if Alison had cracked. Two days ago she would have been raving about the lunacy of sending a child out so soon. Alison was running a finger down the discharges. 'I see the little Cary girl went home.'

'Yes. My God, she was lucky. Just looking at her the night she came in I shouldn't have thought she stood a chance, let alone walk out of here bright as a button. Her memory of the accident and the following day or so is impaired, that's all. Blessing, probably. Oh yes, and her mum and dad called into the office with a box of chocolates for us. I put your share in the fridge. Mr and Mrs Cary are back together again, so something good came out of it, I suppose.'

'I'm glad they are. People should try and forget their differences and love each other.' Alison issued a beatific smile and Chris wondered if she had got religion.

'Yes, well,' Chris said, inclined to be sceptical, 'I had the feeling it was Mrs Cary doing all the forgetting—still . . .' she shrugged, 'I could be wrong.'

But not even Chris's scepticism could dim Alison's happiness, precarious and delicate though she knew it to be. The morning sped past on wings, the doctor's round had gone like clockwork. And Steve—she remembered every look, every smile, every quiet word distinctly—had spent an hour in the office afterwards, going over each patient in detail, discussing treatment, ideas, and arranging for the next lot of admissions. She had done all the essential things around the ward as calmly and as efficiently as always, but with a sense that some other happy, smiling woman inhabited her body. As she paused to consider her condition, the corners of her mouth turned down. She was as euphoric as any young girl on her first love affair.

There was, though, a fair amount of furtive activity going on, and if Alison had been her usual perceptive self she would have noted it. As it happened, she wasn't aware of anything unusual until she was called on to join the others at afternoon tea. She was on the point of declining, always taking tea at that hour quietly in her office while she did the report. Then she thought, why not? and accepted. Molly pushed open the door, and Hine ushered her in.

Everyone began singing, 'Happy Birthday'. It was funny, because at first she thought it was someone else's birthday and she was about to join in. And then she realised.

The entire staff had somehow managed to cram themselves into the small room, even the night nurses were there. And Stuart and Rob were leading the chorus. Alison's eyes flew round the room searching for Steve, the significance of it all beginning to unfold with an agonising edge of reality. Because of the noise, she didn't hear the steps coming in, though she knew his footfall so very well. Or that he was standing right behind her. She was thinking with considerable relief that he wasn't in the room, and they were well into a third chorus before she felt the touch on her shoulder, and had turned and thrown up her hands to cover her face.

Then everybody was calling on her to make a speech. 'How—how did you find out?' she stammered, amidst laughter. For she hadn't told a soul. Not a soul. Of course the information was in the records, but people didn't usually bother to check. And this was one birthday she would have preferred to let slip by without mention.

'Make way there, make way. Come on, Sister, blow the candles out.' Stuart pulled her through the throng to the table where Hine was lighting the candles. Thirty of them. Thirty. To Alison, they looked more like three hundred. Certainly a lot anyway.

'Don't worry,' a wag called. 'Go ahead—blow them out. We've got the fire brigade on standby.' Everyone laughed, Alison among them. But she was thinking that now Steve would know exactly how old she was—if he didn't already. In Alison's opinion, being twenty-nine was one thing, thirty quite another. Though the strange part of it was, a few weeks ago she wouldn't have given it a moment's thought. But now it mattered dreadfully that she was older than he. Knowing how silly that was didn't help much either.

They were waiting for her. Alison took a long deep breath and blew. All but one went out. It flickered stubbornly, then the others gathered round and started blowing and there was a great deal of hilarity. The candles out at last with the hated things removed, Alison cut the cake into slices and started handing around the plates. Steve took his and chided her for not telling him, and she threw off a humorous remark, but didn't quite look at him.

'This calls for a drink at the pub later on,' he said. She didn't answer at first and he wondered if she had heard in the babble around them.

'Thank you, but I—um—I've something else arranged for later.' She smiled up at him, but the long lashes concealed panic. Dear God, and now she had lied to him, because she had nothing planned at all. It wasn't the lie that sent her cheeks flaming scarlet with humiliation, however. It was because she cared for him, so much that she had been prepared to keep the fact she had turned thirty a secret from him.

The phone rang her office and Alison excused herself. Steve was convinced that Trevor Smaille had arranged some kind of birthday celebration, and he glowered after her, momentarily regretting the impulse that had made him ask her to the Hains's party. If he was in his right mind, he should be taking Kirstin.

But Steve Barratt wasn't in his right mind, and that had been obvious for some little time. The impulse that had prompted him to ask Alison instead of Kirstin, he now surmised wryly, was the same impulse that drove him to take her into his arms and wonder, wrongly maybe, that he loved her and what it must feel like to be married—neither Clair nor Kirstin had stirred these sentiments in him. And then Alison was back with news that drove every other thought from his mind.

'We have a bad burns case coming in,' she said quietly from the door. The talking ceased immediately. 'A little girl, three years of age. She'll be here in approximately half an hour . . .' Alison paused, her face reflecting the horror she felt. 'Apparently her parents were frying up fish and chips in their shop and she slipped into the vat of burning oil. She was pulled out almost instantly, but even so, it's thought the burns may be deep enough to involve muscle and bone in some areas.' There was dead silence in the room now, every face showed serious concern. A child's badly burned body was enough to make an angel weep. The pain simply went on and on, day after day, and the nurses who had to carry out treatments that inflicted more were often completely demoralised by it.

'Staff Nurse Manning, you've worked in a burns unit?' asked Alison. Clair nodded. 'Then would you set up the unit and take charge of her care, please. You, Nurse Slade, go straight along to CSSD and get all the sterile equipment.

That will include linen as well. Get a porter to help you bring it back.' She went on quietly delegating and giving instructions, so that within minutes every nurse on duty knew exactly what to do.

Ee-Wyn, when she arrived, was Chinese and very brave. She was accompanied by a coterie of relatives: parents, grandparents, brothers and sisters and several aunts and uncles, all of whom appeared to be in varying stages of grief and shock and could not be expected to comfort the child in such emotional distress. Alison saw to it they were taken under the wing of one of her most experienced staff nurses and settled in the quiet little room kept for such purposes and offered tea and all the comfort and reassurance it was in a nurse's power to give.

Alison helped transfer Ee-Wyn on to a bed in a side room and turned to assist Bob McKenzie put up an intravenous line. While he looked for a site, holding one frail arm up and then the other, flicking at a possible vein and then dismissing it with a frown, Alison prepared the intravenous fluids with one eye on the clock as the vital minutes ticked by in what appeared to be an increasingly fruitless search.

'We need that vein,' Steve observed quietly as he made his rapid assessment of the child's chances of surviving.

'Can't find one,' muttered Rob. 'We'll have to do a cut-down, no other way.' They had to urgently replace the body fluids Ee-Wyn was losing through the large surface area affected by burns, it was their only hope of saving her. Alison was already opening the venesection tray as Steve took Rob's place.

'Draw up some local. Clair, can you splint her arm—that's the way. That sedation we gave her has knocked her out cold. What's her blood pressure like? God. Let's get on with it.' Steve snapped his gloves on and picked up the Bard-Parker handle and inserted the blade.

'Get her wrist over a bit further so the inner malleolus is exposed. OK. Now—the median basilic vein should be right here.' For a second his hand hovered over the site, then he went in.

'Yep, there it is.' Alison was too busy handing instruments to look. Tongue between his teeth, Steve inserted the cannula. He was in. The blood spurted out and Alison was ready to attach the giving set, fingers a little unsteady, her bottom lip caught between her teeth.

'Good girl, you've got it.' His hand was already waving for the suture, he gave instructions for the rate he wanted the fluids as he worked. 'Got a dressing there. Right.' He straightened and squinted at the intravenous bottle before moving away. 'Round one,' he muttered.

Ee-Wyn was to go to theatre to have her wounds cleansed and the loose skin removed under a general anaesthetic. Alison helped Clair to prepare her for theatre. They worked swiftly, keeping their eyes on what they were doing and not talking. Usually someone made a light comment that would relieve the strain, but not this time. There was an aspect about dealing with a casualty of this nature that even the most hardened couldn't face with equanimity. Later on, Steve found Alison in the office, pale-faced and serious.

He looked beyond her through the window and out into the bright afternoon outside, trying to think of something comforting to say. But the words weren't there. He turned to study the information board.

'Once we've debrided the old skin and cleaned her up a bit——' He turned back to face Alison, forgot what he had been going to say and sat down heavily in a chair opposite her desk.

'We've got a Stryker frame,' Alison said. 'Would you want her in one? Or perhaps something else, if we could rig it up. Something like a mesh which would be comfortable to lie on and would increase the air flow. We want to try and keep the bandages dry.'

'Could you do something like that?' Steve asked. 'I'd hate to put a little kid like that into a Stryker.'

Alison thought for a moment. She had control of herself again, and everything in her concentrated on the task that lay ahead. 'Yes, we could,' she said finally. 'I'll get the engineers around, and between us, we should think of something.' For a moment they were silent.

'If the burns are dressed, rather than having them

exposed, it means we don't have to limit the number of people entering the isolation area so much,' Alison said. 'Going on the numer of relatives Ee-Wyn has, that might have been a problem.' Steve looked at her gratefully. He was fully aware of the disciplined effort it took to keep thinking objectively when it concerned a mite as fragile as Ee-Wyn. He sensed that later, Alison would seek out some quiet spot to cry in. He wished suddenly that she would be there for him, when he got out of theatre. But she had her evening arranged, and he wasn't going to spoil that for her—if it wasn't already.

'I'd better go . . .' He paused at the door and looked back at her sternly. 'We'll be a while, so don't go looking for an excuse to wait around. You hear?'

Alison smiled faintly and dropped her eyes. 'I heard.' She picked up the phone and dialled through to the engineers. She had just the thing in mind, and with luck she could get them before they went home.

The evening air was alive with insects as Alison pushed the gate open and paused to linger on the path. She was looking at the garden with new eyes, now that she knew a little something about it. It was surprising just how many flowers there were; the yellow marigold and canna tucked in between the dahlias and splashy gladioli, cool blue hydrangea bushes in the corners, cornflowers and scarlet geraniums along by the verandah and the passion-fruit creeper upon the balustrades and overrunning the pillars. Best of all the exquisite little gentleman's buttonhole roses and sprays of lavender beneath the windows. While by the old concrete water tank at the back door grew the lilac and fragrant verbena. She couldn't think what it would be like now to live without such a garden. Then hearing the rattle of Anne's old Volkswagen, she waited, and was surprised when Kirstin appeared with her. They both carried large boxes festively tied with ribbons.

'Surprise!' they cried, laughingly grabbing her arms, one on either side. Alison looked at each in turn and was pulled up the verandah steps and hustled inside. In the kitchen

Kirstin started taking a bottle of wine from the fridge and Anne opened the boxes to reveal a cake and an astonishing assortment of mouthwatering savouries.

'We raided the deli on the way home,' Kirstin told her, and thrust a glass in her hand and proceeded to fill it. 'Happy birthday . . .'

Alison raised her glass. 'Cheers,' she said, and discovered she was half laughing and half crying. The other two seemed not to notice anything particularly odd and began setting the table for a feast. But it wasn't until much later in the evening, when she had phoned the hospital and found that Ee-Wyn was out of immediate danger and resting comfortably that Alison was able to settle down with anything like peace in her heart.

Alison flung the last remaining dress on her bed. 'Hopeless,' she said, close to despair. Not until she had tried them on and stared in the mirror for long frustrating moments had she realised how positively dreary they all were.

'They do look a bit matronly,' Anne agreed. 'But what about this one?' She held up the soft filmy dress Alison had worn to the McKenzies' barbecue.

'I never got the chocolate stains out,' Alison said. 'Look, you can see them. Here, and here. Oh, dear God!'

'I've got something that would look stunning on you,' Kirstin said quietly. Their friendship had been a tiny bit strained and Alison didn't quite know what to say. 'No, really, I don't mind,' Kirstin said, half aware of Alison's embarrassment. She had to confess, she had been as surprised as anyone that Steve was taking Alison to Gilbert Hains's party, and it had taken her the whole week to get used to the idea. Clair Manning was still very sour about it, though. Every time Kirstin went along to the ward to take Ee-Wyn through her series of passive exercises, Clair had some snide comment to make about Alison. It amused Kirstin the way Clair now looked upon her as an ally.

'Try this,' Kirstin said, coming back with a vivid red chemise draped over one arm. She held it out and Alison gazed at it wonderingly. She had never worn red, or anything quite so daring, come to that. Though it was basically a simple silk sheath with a high Chinese collar, the long fully gathered sleeves were slit provocatively from wrist to shoulder, as was the skirt, Alison noticed when she tried it on—several good inches up the leg both sides.

'Wow!' Anne said admiringly. 'Fits perfectly. Leave your legs bare and paint your toenails. I've got some strappy heels that would be great.'

'She'd better wear the lipstick and nail polish I brought to match the dress,' Kirstin observed, quite unable to take her eyes off Alison.

'You don't think it's a bit—a bit . . .' Alison looked into the mirror and frowned, 'over the top, do you?' Kirstin and Anne shook their heads.

'You'll knock every other woman into a cocked hat,' Kirstin said. When Steve Barratt turned up half an hour later, she let him in with a resigned smile and saw that he thought so as well.

In the car beside him, Alison kept sneaking anxious looks at his face. Worries about being overdressed had receded the moment she had seen the flawless cut of his suit, white dress shirt and smart tie. With his tanned, blond good looks and easy elegance and superb clothes, he looked wonderful. But he hadn't said he liked the way she looked.

'Well . . .' she said at last, 'what do you think?' Steve grinned and changed gears to take a tight corner. He drove a car like a rally driver. Anything else, he always said, was cruising.

'Ravishing . . .' He flicked a glance and caught the long line of bare leg the slit skirt revealed and swallowed. On any other girl, fine. But on Alison? He felt a jealousy and a possessiveness that was quite alien to him. Damn it, if she were his wife, she wouldn't be wearing that dress. He wasn't going to have every man in the room ogling her.

Steve was obliged to keep a watchful eye on her, if not a protective hand lightly at her elbow, for most of the evening; though this was scarcely necessary, as parties frightened Alison quite enough, without finding herself the centre of a surprising amount of attention. Alison was grateful to have him constantly nearby. She sensed an aura of protection and blossomed under its sphere. For Steve, it was an altogether unusual experience; he was accustomed to leaving his partner to fend for herself, while he did the rounds, the perennial bachelor, laughing, flirting, with nothing more serious on his mind than having a good time. Now here he was, scowling if some man stayed at her side too long.

Supper was served in the smart, ultra-modern dining room, from a table laden with hot and cold food of every description. With their plates in their hands, Steve steered Alison out to the brightly tiled patio-pool area, where a few couples were dancing and the rest sitting around where ever a seat could be found. There was hardly a soul Steve knew well, which did not surprise him. The old man kept open house for the Diplomatic Corps and the really wealthy, who only came to Fort William for the deep-sea fishing to be had in the waters of the giant curving bay. From the array of expensive foreign cars he had seen outside the house, his was one of the few local plates there.

'I think we can decently go after supper,' Steve murmured into Alison's ear, during a moment of respite from a lady with rose-tinted hair and diamanté clips on her spectacles who was insisting upon giving him her life story, and whose husband was forever pressing a drink of some description into Alison's hand. Alison nodded. An invisible veil had fallen away from her face, leaving it selfless, prideless, defenceless, in the totality of her love for him.

Gilbert Hains, when they finally located him, was lounging in one of his enormous white leather chairs and chatting with a woman of indeterminate age. 'Not going?' he said regretfully, seizing hold of Alison's hand. Steve said they must, and as Mrs Hains had apparently retired with a headache, they said a few polite words, Alison retrieved her hand, and they made their departure.

'Did you meet the American who comes every year to Fort William just for the fishing?' Alison asked as they drove away.

Steve smiled. 'The one telling all the fish stories? Yeah, I met him.' He took his hand away from the gear lever to cover hers. He had done it unconsciously, she realised, as though he drove her home every night and placed his hand thus in her lap. If only he knew the strange light feeling that came over her when he touched her, the pleasure that diffused her entire body.

They talked very little on the way, and the hand kept returning to her lap after each gear change. Just before they reached the farmhouse, she had almost plucked up the courage to invite him in. She wanted to, and then she didn't. What if Anne and Kirstin were still up? What if they weren't? The joy of having him to herself, and the nervousness.

Steve said suddenly, 'It's not late, come back to my place for a nightcap?' He glanced at her, amused to see her so hesitant, and as they swept past the familiar tall hedge, he chuckled, 'Too late now.' A little way on he slowed and turned the car into a dark bush-lined drive.

'About time we were more neighbourly, don't you think?' And as Alison gasped he looked at her in genuine alarm. 'Now what?'

'But your house . . .' she exclaimed in delight. 'It's lovely!' All the way up the drive, a tangle of strange-looking trees had kept the house hidden from sight, so that she was not prepared for the sudden space of lawns, or the surprising appearance of the house itself. With its delicate fretwork and pillared verandah and high gabled upstairs windows, it looked ghostly white, and as fragile as a wedding cake under the moonlight.

Light streamed from the windows leading to the verandah and from the glass panels of the front door and spilled palely gold on to the lawn. Camellias grew on either side of the verandah steps. Steve led Alison up and across the wooden verandah with its cane chairs and tables and geraniums in pots, and into a large square hall, where a sweeping staircase made its entrance.

'Kauri,' he said, patting the curving banister in passing. 'Built by my grandfather. Come on through to the kitchen and I'll make us some hot chocolate.' He walked her down the hall, a light shifting grip on her arm, his thumb caressing the smooth skin through the slashed silk. All Alison felt now was a perilous weakness—as if her insides had of a sudden turned to pulsating jelly. She realised all at once that the things she had been worrying about were unimportant. The fact that she was thirty, and older than he was, it didn't matter. Or that they were unsuited, or from different backgrounds, or even that he was interested in every pretty girl and seemed not to stay long with any one of them. So long as he was with her, she didn't care about anything else.

The kitchen proved to be large and friendly with a handsome old coal range set into a brick recess. On it was a massive stone jar of arum lilies and their musky persuasive scent pervaded the room. A clock ticked on the mantelpiece, reminding Alison of Montegue Place, the London house she had grown up in and which had been sold after her father's death.

While Steve was preparing the drink, Alison wandered over to the sitting area by the open windows where there was a homely array of comfortable chairs and a long low coffee table covered in magazines and papers. On a small round table was a bowl of daisies and several framed photographs. Alison looked at them curiously. There was one of Steve taken on graduation day, looking heartrendingly young and fresh and handsome, and one with him in tennis shorts sitting with a nice-looking couple who she presumed were his parents. The last photograph showed a girl playing tennis. Her hair was tucked into a band and it wasn't a good snap, or very clear, but she was obviously stunningly beautiful.

'I forgot to tell you,' Steve shoved aside a heap of papers and put the tray down on the coffee table, 'I had a chat with Sue-Ann today.'

'Did you?' Alison got up and went to sit nearer the table, his question effectively putting the girl in the photograph out of her mind. 'What was the outcome?'

Steve pulled a wry face and sat down beside her on the

couch. 'She didn't appreciate me talking to her like a Dutch uncle, let me tell you that. *But* she promised to consider, shall we say, the direction her life was taking.' He grinned. 'I think she's beginning to see her friends for what they are. She wants to be a nurse, she told me. Which means doing a lot better at school than she has of late.'

'I'm so glad . . .' Alison was looking at him with those eyes and Steve had a sudden violent urge to take her into his arms. He had to put all his concentration into what she was saying. It was difficult, she was so close, her head turned a little away so that her profile was caught in the soft illumination of a table lamp.

'Remember that first day?' he asked, after they had discussed Sue-Ann, her problems, Aunt May's leg, the hospital and every other blessed thing. Her expression didn't change, though there was something different in the cool eyes—this enigmatic, shy, intensely vulnerable woman beside him.

Would she ever forget that day when he wandered into her office, his eyes insolent, baiting her, the smile easy, confident? Without knowing it he had changed her life. As simple as that. She had thought him young and conceited and brash. She had found instead a mature, courteous man. A man who talked straight, who didn't tolerate fools easily and who was liable to call a spade a spade, but who was always concerned for people who needed his help. Dislike had turned to love; even though she had found to her cost that to love was to be vulnerable.

She looked up at him and his hand curled around her shoulder. She felt his fingers on her bare skin, stroking, exploring, suffusing her with a curious excitement and a sudden feeling that left her breathless. As her mouth parted, he pulled her violently into the fork of his arm, his free hand was in her hair, pulling it loose. In a sudden frenzy he was ravishing her face with kisses, kissing her until she was crying and half moaning, her body responsive and yielding. He kissed her shoulders and back and then turned and pressed his mouth to the throbbing pulse at the base of her throat.

With sudden violence he stopped, his hands in her hair, tilting her head to gaze into her face. The frightened urgency in her eyes sent the blood pulsing through his veins, he began kissing her, stroking her breasts, knowing he was almost beyond the point where he was capable of stopping. Did it matter? Did anything matter but this sweet vulnerable thing in his arms, her skin flushed and sweet, her whole body trembling. He kissed her shoulders, fumbling at the back for the zip, his hands frenzied, unbearably stimulated by the fire they had lit between them.

'Steve . . .' Her voice was surely not her own. 'Steve, we mustn't.' He closed his eyes as if in pain.

'Why mustn't we . . . if we both feel like this?' He was burning up with fever, he didn't know if he could stop. She was looking up at him, her eyes luminous, her full lips parted as she gasped, her full, tight breasts, heaving. Under that cool exterior was an exciting, sensual woman who needed to be loved and cherished . . .

'Oh God,' he croaked, 'you're right. But don't expect me to agree with you every time.' He held her strongly and tightly in his arms, as if just looking at her face would push him irrevocably over the edge.

'I'll take you home.' He dragged her to her feet, his face rueful. Then he took her by the hands and kissed her smooth high forehead, and the tip of her nose, and led her from the house into the still, moonlit night.

Tucked carefully into the front seat, Alison had her hand relinquished only until Steve was back in the other side. She snuggled down and rested her head on his shoulder.

'Happy?' He bent to kiss her hair before backing the Land Rover round. There seemed no need to talk on the short journey back. There was a bond of understanding between them, and a curious exultation and excitement.

He walked her up the path, and when she turned starry eyes up to his, kissed her lingeringly on the lips, then reluctantly let her go. Alison drifted into the house feeling less in command of her actions then at any time she could remember in all her thirty years.

CHAPTER EIGHT

ALISON looked back along the corridor with a frown, then she walked into the office. 'Morning, Chris. Where's Ee-Wyn's nurse, do you know?'

'What?' Chris stared up from the night report in surprise. 'Sister Prentice, you're early. Er—I think she went along to the kitchen to make the coffee. Anything wrong?'

'Oh, no. But I'm wondering about the extra bed in Ee-Wyn's room, and more specifically, the old gentleman in it?' Alison hitched her shoulder-bag over the door peg and glanced back over her shoulder at Chris. 'Are we running a guesthouse now, or what?'

'That'll be Grandad. He should have gone by now, but I guess they didn't like to throw him out at this hour—he's awfully old.'

'He looks a hundred, if he's a day. For a moment there I thought I was in the wrong ward.' Alison sat down by the desk to wait. She was sure there would be an explanation, and she was curious to hear it.

'You know Ee-Wyn has this large family,' Chris began, and Alison nodded. Every child in the ward came from a large family, it seemed. Even the ones with solo parents could boast an extended one. It was one of the nice things about living in a small town with a supportive community, there was always somebody who could come and visit.

Chris gave an embarrassed smile. 'To cut a long story short, Ee-Wyn hasn't been settling at nights. She misses her family, so somebody comes and stays the night. Then it got so we thought they might as well have a bed and be comfortable.'

'You mean there's been a member of her family sleeping in the room every night and that information was never included in the report? Doesn't the Night Sister do a round any more?'

'Ah. Well, she comes very early. And Mr Barratt said that

131

perhaps until the visiting restrictions are lifted, it might be best to keep mum about it. You know what the top brass are like about rules and regulations.'

Alison did. She looked at Chris, her face losing its brightness. 'But he would have mentioned it to me, surely . . .' Alison stared into space. Surely he would have mentioned a matter so important. She gave her head a shake. 'But Chris, the report for patients on the critical list goes to the Matron and must say who they've been seen by, visitors if any, etc. I know it sounds like endless red tape, but those are the rules. Apart from the fact that I should know exactly what happens in this ward during the night because I carry responsibility for everyone in it, visitors included. What if the grandad had a heart attack and he's found in a bed in our ward? Or there was a fire?'

Chris's face had gone a dull red. She hadn't liked going behind Alison's back. But Clair Manning had insisted that if Sister knew, she'd kick up a fuss and refuse permission, and if the ruling was going to be changed within a matter of days, what did it matter?

Alison got up and walked over to the window. She took responsibility for many things that happened in the ward, some that would not be prudent to reveal to officialdom, for all her resolutions to keep to professional rules. 'Well, heavens above, if the child can't sleep without one of the family being present, then let them be present. But Chris,' she turned, 'so long as I know about it in the future. Understood?'

'Yes, Sister.' Chris grinned and signed her name to the last report and shut the file. 'You're early this morning, though,' she said, as Alison remained standing at the window.

'I couldn't sleep any longer,' Alison admitted. 'The birds woke me up and the sky was rose pink, it was such a heavenly colour. I've never seen a sunrise like it. I simply had to get up.' After Steve had left her the night before, after that rapturous, careless happines, she had spent the night tossing and turning. She was a woman, apparently, who couldn't be happy with the glorious summer days of now, she had to see beyond, to the violent regrets and the dead grey of winter when he had gone. For wouldn't he leave her in the end, as he had left the others? When she woke up, she had been tempted to call him on the phone, just for the reassurance of his voice. Of course she hadn't. What possible excuse did she have for ringing him at that early hour? But she was terribly afraid that she had fallen victim to his easy charm . . .

All this, of course, she couldn't tell Chris, and she turned from the window, frowning. It was very strange that he hadn't said anything about Ee-Wyn's family staying overnight. Had it slipped his mind? Or did he think that now he had her tamed, he could go ahead and make decisions without bothering to consult her? 'I saw the Matron yesterday,' she told Chris. 'I've finally decided the nursing staff can start wearing civvies on the ward on a trial basis and I want everyone's opinion.'

Chris wrinkled her nose. 'Dunno,' she said thoughtfully. 'I can't see the allowance covering the sort of wear and tear we have on our clothes. And there's the laundry costs. We'll have to do our own.' She shrugged and pulled a face. 'But I'm willing to give it a try, I guess.'

Later, when there was a few minutes to spare between giving the report and the doctor's round, Alison explained what she had in mind to the assembled staff. Most were in favour, especially when they heard about the generous-sounding clothes allowance. Only Clair was noticeably lacking in enthusiasm. She knew how well the uniform suited her, and she knew the value of it, when it came to impressing the medical fraternity. Plainly, simple cotton dresses were not in the same league. She glowered intently at her perfect nails, and waited until the others had left to begin their duties before making her comment.

'Steve's done quite a thorough job of buttering you up,' she said nastily, but with a languid stretch of her arms as she got up from her chair. Alison's face had suffused with colour, and Clair stayed a moment to enjoy the sight. 'But if you want it for the record, I for one don't agree with wearing civvies.' She had never mentioned any such reservation to Steve Barratt, never dreaming that Alison would actually give the crazy scheme the go-ahead. But now that she had buckled to and was going along with it, and Steve had taken himself off to pastures new (Alison, by the sound of it), Clair felt she had little to lose, in voicing her opinions. Besides . . .

'It hardly matters what I think,' she added with a shrug, 'because I'm thinking about going to Australia anyway and I'll probably hand in my notice soon.'

It was difficult to forget Clair's jibe, but Alison did her best, and if she didn't manage to summon any warmth to her voice, she did at least sound sincere. 'I'll be sorry to lose you, then, because you're an excellent nurse, as your work testifies.'

Clair found herself flushing with pleasure, and hated Alison all the more. Not knowing what to say, she said nothing. Stalking out of the door, she nearly collided with Steve Barratt on his way in. She threw him a furious glance and turned down the corridor to Ee-Wyn's room. Steve stared after her, then sauntered into the office.

'Trouble?' he asked, smiling his lazy smile, his blue eyes seeking Alison's. He looked unbearably handsome this morning, clean-shaven, the texture of his skin gleaming with health and vitality. The sheer physical power of his presence made Alison glance away with her pulse racing.

'Not really.' She began gathering up folders and pads for the round. 'You'll be happy to know,' she said with a slight smile, 'that we'll be wearing civvies as from next week, for a trial run anyway . . .' Clair's remark niggled in her mind and she dismissed it quickly. The decision had been her own, and only after weighing all the pros and cons, and more especially because she really did think it would bring an informality to the ward that might make the staff look more approachable to those anxious relatives who found the uniforms off-putting.

'Great!' Steve reached for the folders in her arms. 'I'm pleased to hear it. Next thing is to make the visiting hours more flexible. If we can manage it, I'd like one of the side rooms set up so a parent can stay overnight.'

'Speaking of overnight visitors,' Alison said, glancing at him directly for the first time, 'you didn't tell me the arrangement you'd made for Ee-Wyn.'

'Oh lord, didn't I?' Steve adopted an apologetic face and began stacking things on the Kardex trolley.

'Are you sure it wasn't because you thought it best to keep mum about it?' Alison said heavily. She wished he would turn round now and face her, do anything but shuffle the folders about. 'Because I really need to know what goes on in my own ward.'

'Now don't go getting upset,' he said, placatingly, as though she were a child about to make a scene. 'You know what a stickler you are for rules at times. If we were going to break a few, I thought it best you knew nothing about it, that's all.'

Never before had she been so infuriated with him. Never. The fact that she loved him only made her the more angry. 'That's all?' she breathed. 'You go behind my back, issue instructions to my nurses and then have the temerity to walk in here and say it was for my own good!' Her eyes blazed at him. 'It may seem trivial to you, but the report I hand in to the Matron has to be accurate down to the last detail. It's a legal document, and can be used as evidence in a court of law. Until the Hospital Board lifts the ruling about visiting, then I'm obliged to keep within it.'

'Come on, Alison. If the child was dying there'd be no limit to the number of people she could have at her bed, or the hours she could have them in.'

'In which case we seek permission from the Medical Superintendent, and he carries responsibility for anything that should happen. Don't forget about the case recently in London where the mother was giving her child medication, because she didn't think she was getting enough pain relief. The next medication the nurse administered was an overdosage. Remember that?'

'But you don't mind running the risk of that happening, so long as you don't carry the responsibility,' Steve said, his face suddenly grim, and Alison sank down in her chair, caught between the strict rules and ethics the Nursing

Association required her to adhere to—and the freer, more humane, but infinitely risky procedures Steve wanted to see introduced.

'In any case, it was my permission that was given, not yours,' Steve said, breaking a heavy silence.

'But my job on the line,' said Alison grimly. 'And don't laugh—nurses have been dismissed for less. We're expendable, doctors are not.'

'You're overreacting, as usual.' Steve slammed his foot down on the brake lever and swung the trolley towards the door. 'Save me from the English,' he muttered savagely. 'You're all so rigidly conventional you couldn't find your way out of a paper bag.' Suddenly she was a hidebound Pom and he was an upstart Colonial. It was as if last night had never existed.

Alison stood up with a jerk. All right, so long as she knew where she stood. She was so angry, she didn't even feel any pain. It would come, she knew, but while she was angry with him she could keep it at bay. Outside she could hear Jenny Duncan forgetting her sensible ways and positively simpering as she wished the Registrar good morning. Alison stamped out, congratulating herself that she for one wasn't eating out of his hand. To emphasise the point, she stopped to exchange greetings with Rob McKenzie, who had only just arrived, and to listen sympathetically to a problem concerning one of his children. Just long enough for Steve Barratt's blue eyes to narrow into electric points.

'Shall we get on?' he asked, his impatience barely concealed as Rob began to elucidate on the amusing little things his five-year-old had said on the way to school that morning; and earned a surprised look from the others, and a reproachful one from Alison. Usually he was the one with the air of unhurried charm and all the time in the world to listen, while Alison fretted with impatience to get on, and it didn't suit him to have the roles reversed.

'Look, Sister Prentisss, look!' Two small girls ran down the corridor brandishing several sheets of paper. 'Look what I did!' Their squeals and shouts had Steve raising an eyebrow at Alison.

'Vistors at this hour?' he taunted her, but softly.

'Vistors I know about,' she corrected him with a cool look before bending down to admire the crayon drawings. 'They're lovely. Can we put them up on the wall?' She straightened up, smiling. 'This is Ee-Lyn and Ee-Byn, they come every morning to see their sister before going to school.' She looked down at the two. 'But aren't you late?' The girls' giggles whistled through the gaps in their front teeth, they nudged each other and then Ee-Lyn volunteered a confidence.

'Our classs hass got a holiday day,' she lisped. 'We're going to town shopping.' She dug her sister in the ribs and after a whispered consultation they both said goodbye very politely, as they had obviously been instructed. Alison watched them go and waved with the others. Clair Manning came to the door and joined in. Each one must have been wondering if Ee-Wyn's little legs would ever be as straight and sturdy, for they filed very quietly into the room where she lay gently suspended on a mesh hammock. Ee-Wyn had beautiful black eyes like her sisters. But unlike them, hers were the eyes of a child who had lived through too much pain, too early in life.

'You certainly did a good job with this suspension thing,' Steve said after he had spent a moment or two showing Ee-Wyn his finger puppets, and not being able to raise so much as a smile.

'The engineers spent hours getting it right,' Alison told him. She was inspecting the dressing for any moist areas, which would mean taking them down, and this they did not want to do for another ten days if they could help it. Steve was studying the charts and she went over to his side.

'In ten days we'll be able to remove the sloughs from the deep areas, then we'll proceed with the skin grafts. Otherwise . . .' he looked over at the bed, his eyes reflective, 'otherwise she's doing just great. It'll be months, though, before she can go home.' He glanced around the room. 'Who made all the mobiles?'

'Ee-Lyn's class. They've been wonderful. All the

children are taking a great interest. Most of them knew next
to nothing about being in hospital as a patient, and now
they want to hear about it, so their teacher asked if I would
go in and talk to them.'

'And are you?' Steve gave her a sudden look that sent her
heart thudding in her chest.

'I thought it might be a good idea,' she said, moving away
from him with a tiny frown and trying to pretend she felt
nothing. But the anger had faded, and she was as painfully
aware of him as ever before.

'Sister . . .' Clair Manning stepped forward as they were
leaving the room. Alison nodded for the others to go ahead.
'I made all the arrangements for Ee-Wyn's people to stay
overnight. It wasn't Chris. She had nothing to do with it. I
didn't exactly mean to have a bed set up, but the grandad is
so frail, I suppose he looked kind of pitiful sitting in a
chair . . .'

Alison could hardly hide her astonishment. Clair had a
reputation for fading into the background when it came to
carrying the can for any trouble that occurred. 'I'm glad he
was made comfortable,' Alison said drily. 'Just let's know
next time you bend the rules,' she grinned, and stepped out
of the room.

What with one thing and another, the round was now
hopelessly late, and it was morning tea time before they
were half finished. Steve, recovering his good humour, had
fallen back into his easy ways. Alison stopped suddenly and
looked at her watch, then she gave a tiny shrug. 'Why don't
we stop for tea?' she suggested. Steve turned to the others
and grinned.

'Thought she'd never ask.' He smiled at her, laying her
heart bare, and then led the way to the room where they
congregated, stepping carefully over dump trucks and
wooden blocks and small fingers. Alison thought of the tidy
wards of her student days, with their carefully spaced beds
so many feet from each other, blinds so many inches from
the top, the long, bare stretches of polished linoleum, the
children in bed, tidily, no messy quilts . . . She sighed,
looking around. She ought to mention to the nurses that the

children were not allowed their dump trucks inside. They
would end up with a sandpit in the ward at this rate!

Rob caught up with her and shoulder to shoulder they
walked through the ward, Rob's head bent a little towards
her as he effortlessly picked up the thread of his story about
what had been said by whom, on the way to school that
morning. No one seemed concerned that it had more than
half gone already. Was she slipping? Alison wondered as
she listened. Or learning to relax? She lifted up a child who
was bawling professionally and with great artistry, and told
Nurse Slade to straighten her cap.

'But,' the student protested, 'Sister, we won't be wearing
them in a few more days.'

'Never mind, straighten it anyway, it looks terrible. And
take this little one and see what a yoghurt popsicle can do.'
It was no use, the children would only pull it awry again. It
was a game with them. They would miss the caps, Alison
reflected.

Steve arrived unexpectedly at her office that afternoon.
'Alison . . .?' Her hand rose to her throat and rested there,
she stared back at him. 'I've come to apologise. I interfered
in the running of your ward, and I had no right to do that.'
His eyes explored her face.

'Oh,' she said, almost inaudibly. In his characteristic way,
he leant over the desk, precariously near.

'Is that all you have to say? Oh?' he whispered, his voice
tremulous with laughter, flirting outrageously.

Her hand went in a telling gesture to the top button of her
uniform, as if she wanted to make certain it was fastened
securely still. 'That's very nice of you,' she said, her voice
husky, her eyes drawn to his like moths to a flame. She
cleared her throat and dragged them away. 'Actually, I had
a word with Matron. She's given her permission for Ee-
Wyn to have visitors overnight. Though she says, if word
gets round she doesn't quite know how we can refuse other
parents whose children are in long term.' Alison gave a wry
smile. 'But I suppose that's one bridge we cross when we
come to it.'

'And I squared it with the Medical Super.' Steve grinned.
'He was a bit cagey about giving it, he expects that next
parents will be writing to their Member of Parliment if they
don't automatically qualify for a bed for the night.
Especially those who come from out of town. Oh yes, and
by the way, already we've had some expecting to be put up
in the Nurses' Home, apparently.' Alison caught his eye,
and they both laughed.

'Well,' said Alison, 'what can you expect? If visiting
hours are going to be changed so parents can stay in the
ward during the night, the hospital is going to have to
provide facilities for them. Liberal ideas are all very well,
just so long as there is the means to implement them. Take
this movement for home births that's the fashion at the
moment. You simply must have a good back-up system, or
you can't do it. Like in England, we have the Flying Squad
who can be with a midwife attending a delivery, in minutes
of her call. People tend to forget how high the infant
mortality rate was before modern obstetrics.'

Steve had taken a seat on the other side of the desk, and
he listened quietly while her candid gaze swept his face.
Now he leaned forward with his arms folded on the desk,
the strong features of his face relaxed, the little lines of
tension round his eyes softened by a smile. He had the
feeling they were at last on the same wavelength. Probably
always had been. They just approached problems from
different angles. He agreed with everything Alison had
been saying, in fact, he had been trying to get exactly those
points across to the Board. His lips twitched.

'There's a planning session for the new wing coming up
next week some time. I want you, Sister Prentissss,' he
imitated Ee-Wyn's sisters, 'to come along and talk to the
architect. With luck we can get ourselves on to the
committee and tell them what we want . . .'

And suddenly they were in a flood of talk. She would
listen to him and then he would ask a question, sending her
off in another direction until she had to pause for breath.
Why had she never realised before how alike their ideas
were?

Steve leaned back in his chair shaking his leonine head. 'You'll be giving me a soapbox in a moment!' Alison shook her head, eyes dancing, and he smiled back at her. 'I'd almost forgotten what it is I really came to see you about.'

'And I thought you came to apologise,' she said, her brows shooting up with mock fierceness. Steve laughed.

'That goes without saying,' leaning forward again. 'Do you remember that day at the Meeting House?' Alison nodded—how could she ever forget that day? 'And Tiny? Remember that little guy? His old Nana died of a heart attack. The *tangi* is tomorrow—the Maori funeral. I'll be going and Moana wondered if you would like to come as well?' He was smiling at her. 'It's quite an honour to be asked,' he added softly.

'Yes,' Alison said simply. She pulled out the roster and began making rapid calculations. 'I think I can leave the ward well covered.' She looked up. 'What time?'

Steve shrugged. 'If we left by eleven ,we could be back by mid-afternoon—if you can manage that. The funeral will be held on the *marai*, which is the village meeting ground.'

The next day, Alison stood side by side with Steve as part of a large crowd—for it seemed nobody from the village had gone to work that day—and listened to the good English and looked at the modern clothes and the luxurious coffin and the English flowers and pondered the enigma of the two intermingling cultures. This funeral wasn't so very different. But then, as the gathering began on the Maori burial hymn and the casket was lifted into a grave strewn with hundreds of golden chrysanthemums, and a solo tenor's voice pierced the heavens with a lament, the stream of flowers, the lament rising in haunting melody and the weeping and the hair blowing in the wind and the natural dignity of grief, she was overwhelmed. Tears flowed down her cheeks, she clung to Steve's hand, saddened beyond belief as she never had been at her father's funeral. Into eternity she would remember the power of this feeling, the magic, the singing all around her and the fluttering of flowers in the wind, the Minister reading the words; ashes to ashes, dust to dust . . .

She was still clutching Steve's hand on the way back to Fort William, desperately trying to get her emotions under control. 'When they started that singing . . . It was almost unbearable, the pain of it, the sheer beauty, and then . . . I cried my eyes out, didn't I?' she admitted, embarrassed.

He gave her hand a squeeze.

'If I have as good a send-off as old Nana I'd die a happy man,' he said. 'It's important, don't you think, for those loved ones left to grieve, to have the ritual of a burial ceremony. Being able to let the grief flow out. Rather better than locking it inside and taking to valium sandwiches.' He was silent a moment while Alison sat holding his hand as if she never intended letting go. 'Is that what you did?' he asked suddenly.

'I've never taken valium in my life,' she exclaimed, turning to look at him. He was smiling and shaking his head. 'Oh, you mean, did I lock the grief away inside me instead of letting it flow with the tears and the singing?' She settled back against the headrest, looking straight ahead. 'I don't know what funerals are like here, amongst the rest of the population,' she said, 'but I imagine they're not so very different from the funerals we have in England. And you know we don't go into much of an outward display of grief. Oh, I cried—I remember that. But I don't remember feeling anything much. Just a sort of numbness. That would be impossible at a Maori funeral. Today, I think, I cried for my father. I certainly thought of him.' She smiled faintly. 'I think perhaps I feel better too. Not so hard and cold inside. Not like perpetual winter.' Steve was driving very slowly and she was content to sit quietly and enjoy the warmth and comfort of his presence, the feel of his thumb caressing the palm of her hand.

'Alison, can I ask you a personal question?' he asked quietly, and she looked at him in surprise, and then nodded. 'Is there anyone else?'

'You mean . . .' She paused, staring at him, all eyes.

'Smaille? Or someone in England you're waiting for?' He

took a quick sideways glance, the look searching.

Alison shook her head, 'No,' she answered quietly. He turned to look at her again, his eyes dark, a question in them.

'But there was?' It was more of a statement than a question. No longer did the memory of James torment her, but memory loosens tears, and suddenly she was weeping. The sort of weeping that was uncontrollable. All this crying, it only ended in a bout of ignominious sniffing, with her make-up all washed off and eyes red from grief. She dabbed at her shiny nose with a sodden tissue. Steve slowed and pulled down a tiny gravel road leading to a stream, coming to rest eventually by a line of poplars. He leaned across and pulled her into his arms.

'Why don't you tell me about it?'

He was gentle, tender, and Alison felt herself responding in a way she could never have imagined. It all came pouring out—things she had never told anyone. The anger and rage at first, and then the pain. She wasn't the first woman to be jilted on her wedding day. But the pain was real, and it didn't discriminate. How she could have expected love to be without it, she couldn't imagine. It terrified her to think of going through anything like that again.

'It's not love that terrifies you,' Steve murmured, his mouth pressed hard against her hair. 'It's the fear of rejection you can't bear to think about. Anyway, the man was a fool. He must have been.' He wound his arms tight about her. 'But I'm glad you didn't get married, because if you had I would never have found you, never . . .' Then his lips were seeking hers.

His wonderful, marvellous words kept echoing in her mind and she felt a sob rise up in her throat. She could no more stop herself from loving him than stop breathing. Whatever came of it, she would have to take the consequences. Her whole body burned for him, she parted her lips and felt the indescribable ecstasy of his hands caressing her ever closer towards the irresistible final moment of surrender when she would lose her senses completely and be one with him.

'Lord,' Steve muttered, 'don't look now, but we're surrounded.' His body was throbbing with passion and he had trouble breathing, but what could he do with a ring of faces looking in at them?

'What?' exclaimed Alison, opening her eyes and staring wildly about. 'Ooooh . . . Ooooh!' She started laughing until she couldn't stop and Steve had to thump her so hard she started coughing; for they were being regarded stolidly by a herd of curious cows. Then came the staccato barking of the dogs and the mournful beasts regretfully lumbered off.

'They're on their way to be milked,' Steve mumbled. 'We'll have the farmer along next.' He was trying to do frantic things in the mirror with his unruly hair. Alison giggled.

'I hope I'm not looking as indecent,' she teased.

'That can be arranged,' Steve said threateningly, and grinned wickedly. 'But maybe we'd better slip away while the going's good, eh?'

They were silent for most of the way back to town, content with wordless communication and deeply aware of the bond that had sprung between them. Steve glanced at Alison several times, compelled by some quality in her face. All the tension and the hurt had dropped away, leaving a pure, defenceless beauty. All he felt was a hot stinging protectiveness towards her. He thought he had been in love many times before, but this was different.

As they turned into the hospital grounds, he glanced at his watch. 'It's rather later than I thought. You want to call it a day and let me drive you home?'

Alison smilingly shook her head. 'There are several things I have to do. I know the ward wouldn't fall apart if they weren't seen to, but it would worry me nevertheless. And I do have my own car,' she reminded him.

'Give it a well earned rest. Do what you have to, and I'll attend to some work of my own, then why don't you come back to my place for dinner? I happen to know Kata has made something special for tonight. Otherwise I'd suggest a meal out, though dressed as we are for a funeral, perhaps that's not the best idea.'

'I like the first suggestion best anyway,' Alison said. Somehow it was tacitly agreed that he would bring her to work the next day. Beyond that, Alison never thought to question. It didn't seem to matter any more.

'Anything been happening?' Alison asked the senior staff nurse on duty.

'Just the usual. We've had one acute, though—Rangi King. Remember him? Youngster from Keina Island?' The nurse handed over a folder of notes.

Alison frowned. 'Not another bout of pneumonia?' She pulled out the notes Rob McKenzie had written and studied them. 'Lobar pneumonia,' she read, and looked at the shaded in areas of Rob's diagram. 'Oh no!' She glanced at the time he was admitted. 'Just after twelve. About the same as last time. I suppose he was brought in on the back of the horse again?'

'I did see Hine feeding Bess some sugar lumps,' the nurse said thoughtfully, 'so I guess that's how he came.' Alison raised an eyebrow but refrained from making any comment.

'Has the physiotherapist been along to give him some postural drainage?' she asked, already busy checking the treatment charts.

'Yes, Sister,' the nurse said smartly, sensing that Alison was becoming less relaxed by the minute.

'Rangi was ordered a broad spectrum antibotic and I see he's been administered a different type. Any reason for that?' Alison looked up. 'I hope it wasn't given in mistake.'

'Oh, no, Sister,' the nurse said, fully alert now. She was thinking that when Prentice liked, she could really make waves. 'We couldn't get the one Dr McKenzie prescribed from Pharmacy and so he said it was all right to go ahead and give what he had in stock.'

'All right,' Alison said quietly, 'but you must get Dr McKenzie to rewrite the order, and you'll need his signature alongside the antibiotic given. Don't call him out this evening, but get him to do it next time you see him, otherwise you're not covered. You do realise that? Anything goes wrong, a reaction to this type of antibiotic and you'd have a job explaining why you'd given it and not the one charted and signed for.' She smiled at the nurse, a fairly young, inexperienced girl, who blinked back in surprise.

'But Dr McKenzie would never let me take the blame, not when he said . . .'

'No, I'm sure he wouldn't,' Alison said quickly. 'But not everybody is as nice or as honourable as Dr McKenzie. Always remember, you give only what's charted. If it's changed, or you take the order over the phone, get it in writing and get it signed. Unless it's down in black and white, legally you don't have a leg to stand on.'

'Who hasn't a leg to stand on?' Steve came into the office with a cheeky grin on his face. His eyes roved down the nurse's pert figure. 'Well, I can see you still have a pair.' The nurse blushed prettily and twiddled with her honey-coloured curls. It was a small thing, but Alison felt claws tear at her stomach. Was she going to feel this way every time he looked at a pretty girl? She hoped not. It was bad enough being at least ten years older than this staff nurse, how would she feel in another ten?

'Rangi King is back in,' she said, turning away. She was feeling the early start, earlier this morning than usual, the long day, the emotion, the crying, her age.

'I've just been to see him. Why has Rob got him on this antibiotic?' Steve held up the treatment chart. Alison explained, and he muttered something rude under his breath about the Pharmacy Department and shook his head. 'I want this changed. Have you rung round the other wards, Nurse?' he asked, and when she shook her curls, he said, 'One of them is bound to have a supply. You ring round and ask if we can borrow a few ampoules.'

Alison left them to sort it out and slipped off to do a round of the ward, walking quietly, tucking a bare arm under the covers here and picking up a pillow and a discarded toy there, getting the inevitable drink of water for a child who wasn't thirsty, as much as he wanted the reassurance of a kiss and a cuddle. She stopped by Rosa's bed, changed her nappy and put her into dry pants, then jiggled the mobile of hopping rabbits until the child's eyelashes drooped heavily on her cheeks. In Ee-Wyn's room she stopped for a chat with two aunts who seemed, she noticed, well settled for the evening, if not for the night. The empty bowls and lingering smell of oriental food suggested that Ee-Wyn was being fed from home. But when the child was gaining weight and recovering in strength by the day and sleeping peacefully at night, who was she to interfere? If it works, leave it alone, she thought, leaving the room and the two aunts with a smile.

Rangi King was another matter. He was a little boy who wasn't thriving, and something would have to be done. Alison stopped by his room to observe the child's rapid shallow breathing and emaciated features with worried eyes. There was nothing, however, she could do at the moment, that wasn't already being done, and when Steve appeared at her shoulder and drew her away, she left without a murmur. Though Rangi would never be far from her thoughts in the days to come. She had to find the solution that would give him the boost in health he needed, even if it meant sending him for several months to one of the excellent children's health camps until he was strong again.

'Comfy?' Steve put out an arm so Alison could rest her head on his shoulder. They had eaten Kata's delicious steak and kidney pie and rhubarb crumble and were curled up with a glass of wine on the shaggy wool rug by the fire. Though the days were lovely and could still be very hot, the nights were drawing chill, and anyway, a pine-cone fire was still an undreamed-of luxury for Alison. She thought, sometimes, it would be impossible to live back in England. She had begun to get a feel for this country. It was becoming home to her.

'Listen—there's a storm getting up,' Steve murmured in her ear. She snuggled closer, listening to the wind in the old macrocarpa tree roaring in the topmost branches, bending them this way and that, until it creaked like the timbers of an old sailing ship.

'Why don't your parents live here?' she asked, wondering how anyone could leave such a lovely old house.

'Mum wanted something modern, with all conveniences, and no stairs, so they built over Hamilton way. Dad's as happy as a sandboy with his horses. Now he's retired he can devote all his time to them. He used to breed them, now he only keeps a few. They live the life of Riley, those horses.' Steve laughed and began kissing her forehead. 'Tell me about you. About when you were a little girl.'

Alison raised her face to him and he stroked her flushed cheeks and kissed her, then suddenly he was kissing her passionately, caressing her with shaky hands.

'Stay with me, darling,' he moaned into the hollow of her throat. He could feel her breasts through the thin cotton top, hard against him. Deeply aroused, slipping further and further into the dark nadir of passion, Alison could no longer find the power to resist him. As his fingers explored and brought an exquisite agony she felt her body surrendering to his maleness. She knew she had only to lift her mouth to his.

'I could take you back home before everyone else is awake. Nobody would ever know.' His blind impulse was to make love to her on the rug in front of the fire and his impassioned body was ready to slip into her soft satiny embrace. But he held himself back forcibly. It had to be what she wanted.

But what he proposed seemed to Alison furtive, somehow, underhand. She wanted Steve as much as he wanted her. But not this way. His words trickled through her mind like cold water. And suddenly all the old suspicion was back. How many other girls had succumbed in the fever of the moment, to be discarded like last season's fashions?

She sat up suddenly, struggling out of his arms, and sat for a moment with head bent, her hair tumbling down over her shoulders in undulating waves, and fought for some measure of control. Clear thinking was almost impossible. What a traitorous thing a body could be! Half dazed, she got to her feet.

'Wait a moment.' Steve shot to his. 'Where are you going? Darling, I said I'd see you safely home early as you want.'

She looked up bravely into the full beauty of those blue eyes. 'I know what you said, but Steve, I can't.'

For a moment he was too stunned to think beyond the blank void of disappointment. More than disappointment— anguish. He was unbearbly aroused and she was going to walk off and leave him. Alison began straightening her clothes, her face red now with embarrassment at the state she was in; trembling still, shaking at the knees, her hair dishevelled and hanging down over her face.

He shrugged. 'The lady says no, that's OK. Your prerogative.' His words were clipped. He glanced at his watch. It was curious, but he'd had the feeling it was so much later, as if his feeling for her had obliterated every other thought from his mind, including his sense of time. He tried to lighten up a little. 'Well,' he said with a half grin, 'we'll both get an early night at this rate, do us good.'

'You're not angry?' Alison asked, feeling miserable now that she had lost the comfort of his strong arms, and sick at the thought she might lose him altogether.

'I'm a lot of things at the moment. But no, angry is not one of them.' Steve reached for his discarded sweater, dragged it on and felt for the car keys in his back pocket. 'But you'd better let me get you home before I'm tempted to kiss you again.'

His voice was warm once more and Alison let out a long breath of relief. It would have been easy to give in, as much to her own feelings as to his, but she hadn't, and she knew instinctively it was something she would not regret. There was a right time. And this wasn't it.

Outside, the wind blew her hair into tangles and stripped the petals from the last of the summer roses and filled her mouth and nostrils with small pieces of cut grass. Summer was about to give way to autumn.

The blinds at the upstairs windows were banging, the curtains fluttering out through the narrow openings. 'I'll have to shut the house up when I get back,' Steve said.

'We're in for a real old storm, by the look of it.' He opened the door. Alison took one last look at the house, and got in.

CHAPTER NINE

'YOU THINK that men respect women who won't fall into bed with them out of principle?' Alison lay on a big striped towel with her head on her arms and lazily studied the little triangles of light cast through her straw hat.

Anne reached for her sun-glasses before sitting up to look at the deserted beach. 'They don't like to think she has with anyone else, that's for sure. But when it concerns them? Seems to me it becomes something of a different matter.' Her voice held an odd flat note and Alison cautiously raised her hat an inch. Anne had a past, she was convinced, but it remained something of a mystery and questions were not invited. 'Where's Steve this weekend?' Anne asked after a moment.

'Visiting his parents.' Alison ran the fine white sand through her fingers. 'Did you ever get to meet them?'

'They'd moved from the district before I arrived. Kirstin would have, I expect.' Anne pushed her shades back on her head and settled on one elbow. 'You'll meet them before long, I bet, the amount of times you two have been seeing each other, and I don't mean at the hospital.'

Alison smiled, but she chose to ignore the gentle probing and closed her eyes, listening to the plop of waves on the sand and thinking back over the last two weeks. Two wonderful weeks, and each morning waking up more deeply in love. It was an incomparable feeling. She knew Steve loved her. He had never said it, not in so many words. Sometimes words were not necessary, she thought contentedly.

Thinking of the little candlelit dinners, the picnics in the long evenings when they were both off duty, the seaside walks, it was easy to forget what had prompted her question to Anne in the first place. Why, and Alison hugged the thought to herself, they had become an established couple, and if Clair hadn't accepted it with as good a grace as she might have, there had at least been no unpleasantness. Anne, of course, was delighted. Only Kirstin had been rather quiet. But then she had gone away on a course for a week, returning the day before as bright and friendly as ever.

'It's so lovely here,' she said, sitting up to look round at the pohutukawa trees on the hill behind them where the sheep were slumbering in the shade.

'Hardly anyone knows about this little beach. Kirstin brought me here. There's another little cove round the other side of the hill, but you can only get to it with a four-wheel-drive.' Anne settled down again, prepared to doze in the warm sun. But Alison felt restless.

'I think I'll walk up to the top,' she said, scrambling up. Anne mumbled something that sounded like 'good luck' and Alison set off. She followed one of the dusty little trails the sheep used and, halfway, turned to look at the sleepy sea. There was no wind, only a faint stirring, and the occasional snapping of a twig as the sheep sought refuge from the midday heat deeper in the bushes. She pressed on. As she gained the brow of the hill, a faint welcome breeze came as a relief, lifting the strands of her hair and fanning it out behind her.

The sea glittered below her and rolled up on to a perfect little beach. She sat down, entranced, her chin resting on her knees. Something caught her eye and she turned her attention lazily to an outcrop of rocks, and it was then she saw the two swimmers. She watched their progress until her eyes ached with the brightness of the sea and then she stretched out on her back on the long, sweet scented grass and gazed up at the faraway, pure blue sky. When next she sat up she saw the man was carrying his companion out of the water. She saw—oh, how plainly—that the man was Steve. The slender girl in his arms had her own around his neck, her short-cropped fair head against his shoulder. Alison sat paralysed, some dark corner of her mind cried out, but all she could do was watch. Watch, as he strode through the leaping sea and up the lovely beach where she saw now an umbrella half hidden in the waving grass behind the dunes.

Alison sat on, trapped in a dark labyrinth of pain, long after there was nothing to mark that the intimate little cove was inhabited. Then she crept away, furtively, as though she were committing some crime simply by being there.

She slithered down the hill until she was running wildly, hair flying loose, catching on the bushes, but uncomprehending, she plunged on. At last she flung herself down under the twisted branch of an old tree and cried until she thought her heart would break. When the spasm of pain had subsided, she lay still, face buried in the rough grass, the dry sandy soil in her mouth and nostrils.

She blamed herself. Falling in love, she had given Steve the responsibility for her own happiness. She had chucked reason and good common sense out with the bathwater. She had given away too much, expected much too much. What had made her think she could hold him, when other, prettier girls had failed? And it wasn't as if she hadn't always known how attracted he was to Kirstin—for she was certain that was who she had seen in his arms.

But she had to stop crying, pull herself together, because Anne would be waiting for her, and she couldn't turn up with a tear-stained face. She would be subjected to questions as yet too shocking and merciless to answer. She sat for a while, her head against the gnarled old trunk, her mind seething, the new pain reinforcing the old.

Fortunately Anne was swimming when she got to the bottom. Alison chucked off her shorts and top and ran into the water. When they got out she spent a long time drying and towelling her hair, so that by the time she was finished, her face simply had the pink scrubbed look of someone who had been swimming in salt water, and Anne anyway was too busy packing up to notice anything wrong.

Driving back along the lonely coastal road, Alison was sick with apprehension that they would be overtaken by the Land Rover. She didn't think she could bear Anne's exclamation of surprise, and an image of Kirstin turning round, smiling and waving, made every nerve in her body jump. But there was no sign. Why should there be? Alison thought drearily, as they gained the comparative safety of the main road; it was far too nice an evening to come back early.

Propped against a glass of nasturtiums on the kitchen table was a note. Anne picked it up. 'It's from Kirstin,' she said. 'Gone for a picnic . . . Not to worry if I'm not back tonight . . .' Anne smiled and glanced at Alison, her expression instantly changing to concern.

'What's the matter? You're as white as a sheet!'

'Oh . . . it's just a headache.' That was true enough, Alison felt as if thunder was hammering in her head. 'Too much sun, I guess. I'll take a couple of tablets and go to bed. Don't worry.'

'You sure? I don't mind staying in this evening if you're not feeling well. I could make some scrambled eggs. We haven't eaten much today . . .' Anne was already at the fridge, her face registering solicitude. Alison repressed a desire to scream. All she wanted was to be left alone. She didn't want anyone fussing, the thought of food made her feel ill.

'No, really, thanks all the same. I'll go up and have a sleep and get something for myself later. You go and see the film, it's only on for another two nights and you don't want to miss it.' At last she had Anne convinced and she was free to go to her room. For good measure, she took three tablets and tossed them over. A few weeks back she had been furious at Steve insisting that she take two, and here she was swallowing three and hoping she could blot out the night with sleep. Not even bothering to shower, she slipped between the covers and buried her head in her pillows. Distantly she heard the phone ring. A few moments later, Anne popped her head round the door.

'Sorry—I said you'd gone to bed with a headache. But he was so insistent . . .'

Alison was already out of bed. It hadn't been Steve on the beach. What a fool she had been to even think . . . She ran down the stairs, snatching up the receiver. 'Hello,' she said unsteadily, her heart in such an uproar she could hear it pounding.

'Alison? Is that you?'

She stared blankly at the wall. It simply hadn't entered her head that the call would be from somebody other than Steve. The disappointment was almost too cruel. 'Yes, Trevor, it's me,' she said, her voice toneless. Anne paused at the front door to wave goodbye, and Alison automatically lifted her hand. Trevor was talking about the weather, he was planning a barbecue the next day and wondered if she would come.

'Alison, Alison—you still there?'

'Yes, sorry. No, thanks all the same, I won't be able to come tomorrow, I've made other arrangements. Yes, yes, soon—I'd like that, thanks again. Goodbye, Trevor.' She hung up and made her uncertain way to the kitchen to pour half a glass of brandy. She couldn't remember it hurting quite this much the last time. Maybe it got worse, as you got older. Or maybe she loved Steve just that much more. And now it was bad, and as the loneliness closed in, she found herself wishing Anne had stayed. Desperately she wanted the comfort of someone near her, someone familiar and comforting she could confide in.

She woke at six on a miserable wet Sunday morning wondering how she was going to get through the day. Anne was working, and Alison spent most of it moping round, unable to leave the house in case the phone rang, and unable to settle, in case it did. She dreaded Kirstin's return. What if Steve came in with her? Even he wouldn't have the gall to do that. Eventually she made the effort and set about making an enormous meal and had it ready for Anne when she got home from work.

As soon as they had washed up, she pleaded tiredness and escaped to her room, hoping to dodge Kirstin when she came in, for surely she would be back on a Sunday night for work the next day. Unless Steve was going to run her into the hospital the next morning?

She lay stiffly in bed in the dark. It seemed hours before she heard the front door bang, and Kirstin's voice in the hall. Anne's room looked out to the front—if she ran through, one glance would tell her whether the Land Rover was outside or not. She fought against the impulse. In any case, he wouldn't want to embarrass her by stopping. But oh, in the hot silence, how her ears strained for any sound of an engine!

Ten minutes later the phone rang and sheer desperation drove her out to the top of the stairs. She heard Anne saying, 'I think she's asleep, Steve, hang on, though, and I'll go and check . . . Oh, here she is now.'

'Thanks, Anne.' Alison took the phone with a glittery smile. She wondered what sort of story they had concocted. She could imagine them discussing it. It would be Steve's job to ring and tell her, of course. 'Hi . . .' she said briefly, the breath catching in her throat. She heard his rich warm chuckle with an intense little pain.

'Hi yourself. You're in bed early tonight. Anne tells me you had too much sun yesterday?' Alison leaned her forehead against the wall and closed her eyes.

'I think I must have. How are your parents?'

'They're fine . . .' Did she imagine a slight pause? 'But listen, I called because Moana wants me to see the schoolchildren in her area, and I thought tomorrow would be a good day. There's nothing Rob can't cope with at the hospital—perhaps you could get away and come along too. What do you think?'

Of course. The ride out would give him an ideal opportunity to talk. Let her down gently, get her into the right frame of mind so there would be no scenes. He must just about have it off pat by now. Did the others feel the same pain? she wondered, and thought, never, never, never would she go through this again.

'I won't be able to, but you go.' Her lips were so stiff she had difficulty in speaking.

'Alison . . .' There was a sudden sympathy in his voice. 'Are you badly sunburnt?' She nearly caved in. She wanted to ask him what had happened. That she had only just begun to believe he cared about her, that he had broken her heart.

But then her heart and her happiness were her own responsibility. Not something to be thrown out to tender, like so much emotional baggage. She swallowed and took a pull on herself. 'No, of course not. My lips are a bit sore, that's all.' She even thought of other things to say. Afterwards, she couldn't remember what they talked about. Kirstin was in the kitchen when she rang off. Alison heard her laughing as she chatted to Anne. Wondering bleakly if it would be possible for them to live in the same house, she slipped back up the stairs, and for the first time in years took a couple of sleeping tablets.

Thank God, it was Rob McKenzie and not Steve doing the doctor's round, Alison thought, as for the second time she had to go back to the office for an item she'd missed from the Kardex trolley. The sleeping tablets had left her with a fuzziness several cups of strong coffee had been unable to dissipate. Apart from that, she felt calm—empty as the blue sky she had lain under on Saturday, but calm. When she got back, Rob and Stuart were tying a line of brightly coloured cardboard clowns across the room, and the ping-pong balls, attached to the clowns' hats by some ingenious device, were making Ee-Wyn chuckle with delight. Smiling, Alison handed the latest lab results over to Rob, who took them, then turned to take a second look at her.

'I'm not used to you in civvies yet,' he said, his eyes inspecting her fully. 'I keep expecting someone in starched white.'

'You think it's a success, then?' Alison looked down at the Liberty print smock she had on over a powder-blue blouse. The nurses were free now to wear anything they chose, so long as it was of a simple style and laundered well. Most had chosen to wear cotton skirts and tops, though Alison was prepared for jeans in the cooler weather. And why not? They were sensible and hard-wearing.

'It still feels very strange to me,' she said, when Rob had given his unqualified approval. 'I keep looking for a nurse. Molly was right under my nose the other day and I never saw her. But probably that's because she looks like one of the kids herself.'

'It's the visitors here all hours I can't get used to,' Rob admitted. 'I'm always being collared. The dads are the worse. Wish I had Steve's knack of doing the expedient.'

'Expedient?' queried Alison, frowning. 'That means being more politic than just, doesn't it?' She shook her head. When she first met him she might have thought so, but not now. Steve Barratt weighed a more complicated set of balances in his mind. He was never merely expedient when it was simply advantageous to him. As a means to an end perhaps, but only when being so benefited his young patients.

'We'd better move on,' she said suddenly, aware of the time. 'I've got Rangi's dad coming in to see me.' But Rob was slow enough to get even Stuart and Jenny irritable, and eventually Alison had to excuse herself when she saw a tall man edge diffidently through the swing doors and stand holding his snap-brim hat in both hands.

'Beg pardon, miss,' he said as Alison hurried up to him, 'I'm looking for Sister.' Alison told him who she was and smiled at his look of mild astonishment.

'We don't wear uniform any longer,' she said, ushering him into the office. 'Would you like a cup of tea?'

'Mighty nice of you. Reckon I would. Thanks.' He eased himself into the chair Alison indicated and waited for her to begin.

Alison had planned what to say very carefully. Rangi's family were proud. They refused to accept the Government allowance they were entitled to, and any suggestion of charity would be declined with thanks. If only Steve were here, he would know the right way to make the suggestion.

'What kind of camp?' Mr King asked warily, after listening to Alison with a disarming wistfulness. He stirred his tea, not once taking his eyes from her face.

Unguarded, Alison said, 'It's a health camp . . .' and knew instantly she had said the wrong thing. A health camp implied that the State thought he couldn't take care of his own child. Mr King wasn't having any of it.

'Soon's the boy's ready he can come home,' he said, standing up. Alison had no choice but accompany him to the door and accept his polite words of gratitude for Rangi's care. After he had gone she returned to her chair and flung herself into it. What a mess she had made of that!

'Anyone at home?' Kirstin's curly head came round the door. 'Mm, any tea left in the pot?'

Alison frowned. 'It's not very fresh,' she muttered as Kirstin converged on the pot and began pouring herself a cup. The white short-sleeved uniform showed off an incomparable tan, something about the perfect quality of her skin destroyed what was left of Alison's equilibrium. 'Anne said you weren't feeling so hot?' Kirstin sipped her tea and studied Alison's face with a searching eye. Her calm friendly manner only made Alison feel more emotionally unstable.

'Did she?' Alison said finally. 'I was feeling sick. I still am. Oh . . .' she flung her hands about desperately, 'I can't be angry with you, Kirstin. He can spend his time with anyone he pleases. God knows, it wasn't as if he promised anything to me. It's my own fault, I knew what I was doing.' She laughed in a cracked sort of way. 'I'm old enough, good heavens. I knew he'd never take a woman seriously. Not seriously enough to commit himself to anyone in particular. It was ludicrous of me to think I stood a chance in hell.' Kirstin stared, her large blue eyes open to the fullest.

'What are you talking about, girl?' she asked, as Alison floundered on, close to hysteria.

With her head lowered, Alison said, 'I wasn't spying. It was just that I happened to be up on the hill overlooking the beach. Anne and I were round in that little cove . . .'

'I know where you were,' Kirstin said, exasperated, 'Anne told me. But anything else I don't know. I went to Rotorua for the weekend with friends of mine, so would you care to explain?'

'But . . .' said Alison, wildly losing all composure. 'But who . . .?' Intoxicated by a ridiculous hope, she rapidly explained.

'Oh, I bet that would be Trish.' Catching the distraught look on Alison's face, Kirstin hastily added, 'Steve's sister, Patricia—and I can see by the look on your face he hasn't told you about her.' Alison shook her head slowly, her eyes unwaveringly on Kirstin's face.

'Well, it's not my place, but I'm going to. He's such an old silly, really. But you have to know some time. It was because of Trish that he came back from England when he did. She wrapped her car round a lamp-post and came out of it with spinal injuries that paralysed both legs.'

'She's a paraplegic,' Alison whispered, the beautiful fair-haired girl playing tennis in the photograph coming back to her. Kirstin nodded. 'But who looks after her?' Alison asked.

'Private hospital, very exclusive. Steve visits, and her parents, that's all. She won't see anyone else. I asked him once, and he said she can't bear the pitying looks people give her. I knew that he took her swimming in the sea sometimes—only isolated places, though. They're very close, always have been. He thought the world of his sister. She was very bright, went to a lot of parties, popular—and he can't seem to come to terms with what's happened. It's as if he shuts that part of his life away in a separate compartment, because he doesn't talk about her any more, to anybody. Isn't that strange?'

'Strange?' Alison echoed wildly. 'It's terrible. And I had no idea. I felt so close to him, I thought I was, and he never mentioned her, never.'

'Not close enough to trust him, apparently.' Kirstin put down her teacup, her eyes were accusing.

Alison flushed. 'If you'd seen him carrying a girl over the sands on a deserted beach when he was supposed to be visiting his parents miles away, what would you think?' she asked. But she did feel ashamed. She could have at least asked him first before she jumped to conclusions, as if she couldn't wait to condemn him. Perhaps she didn't trust him? What sort of future did that hold?—if there was going to be a future, she reminded herself. It was something else Steve had never mentioned.

'Think . . .? Hell, I'd have been waiting for him with my father's old Army rifle,' Kirstin told her, grinning widely.

'But this isn't getting the baby bathed.' She dragged a list from her pocket, pausing first to look at Alison's depressed face. 'Cheer up! It wasn't me in his arms, it was his sister. Now, I'd better scoot and see young Rangi, he's being a bit lax about his breathing exercises. Can you remind your staff to encourage him, he needs someone at him the whole time.'

After Kirstin had gone Alison tried to get on with her work, but her concentration was lost. She felt as if she was crying inside for the terrible thing that had happened to his sister. But why had Steve not told her? She had the conviction that if he really loved her, was even the smallest bit serious about his intentions, he would have confided in her. That he hadn't needed to share that part of his life, hadn't wanted to, left her feeling cold.

Unutterably depressed, Alison slammed the paperwork into her top drawer and went out to help in the ward. If ever there was a cure for the blues, it was here; working with children whose problems were appallingly real, and yet were borne stoically and completely without self-pity. Stuart Dalgleish found her hoisting Rosa into a contraption of braces that hung from a tree in the play area.

'Thought I'd find you out here.' He helped Alison buckle one of the straps and for a moment they stood watching Rosa enjoy a freedom of movement not normally possible for her. 'Great that Steve got the consultancy,' he said, giving Rosa a little push that sent her off gurgling with pleasure.

It was common knowledge that Steve Barratt had applied for the consultant appointment—a mere formality, most agreed—and Alison had been expecting to hear at any time. Stuart slowly became aware of her blank look. 'You didn't know? Heck, I'm sorry, I'm sure Steve wanted to tell you himself.'

'Never mind. I'm just so pleased for him,' Alison said, trying to cover her confusion. 'But how did you find out?

Steve's out at Swampy Creek.'

'He was. Right now he's in the common room celebrating. Why don't you give yourself a tea-break and come on round?' Alison promised she would, and produced the hearty smile that was expected of her.

He was here, in the hospital, and he never came to tell her. The thought hammered at her, giving her no peace, far worse than the noise from the sandpit where the children, newly admitted that morning for Ts and As the next day, were playing. She had expected too much, there was no reason why he should go out of his way to seek her out. Well, she would survive. She would have to, Alison told herself grimly.

She saw the glass of wild flowers the moment she entered the office: buttercups and Queen Anne's lace and daisies and thick flowery orchard grass. She stopped where she was, hands clasped, and then she saw the note underneath and snatched it up. It had 'For Sister Prentice' scrawled along the top in Steve's bold handwriting. 'Got the job. Come and have a drink—you'll find us in the common room.' And it was signed, Steve. That was all. But it was enough to send her reeling. She buried her face in flowers, smelling the fresh fields, the green river at Swampy, and the memory of his kisses—in a flash she was happy again.

The paperwork could wait for the next day, she was at the little mirror behind the door dabbing at her hair. As an afterthought she clipped several buttercups alongside the pleat and applied another coat of lipstick. There—she stood back, her face radiant, her doubts a thing of the past. How easily they vanished.

The common room was crowded. It seemed everyone had turned up to congratulate Steve. Seeing him standing in the midst of so many people, laughing, tanned, his blond hair tousled, so vital and ruggedly masculine, Alison thought, oh God, how she loved him; and suddenly she was all vulnerability again. And then he had seen her.

'Alison . . .' She felt the ecstasy of his strong grasp and her fears melted as he drew her into the crowd, shielding her, protecting her with his strength. With his warmth and humour she was no longer an outsider, but part of him.

'Congratulations,' she murmured as he bent his head for a quick kiss on the cheek. The slight stubble of blond whiskers pricked her skin. He hugged her with his one free arm.

'Like the flowers?' he asked, and she nodded, brimming over with happiness. 'Moana sends her love, so does Tiny,' he whispered. Kirstin wriggled her way through to join them and congratulate Steve by throwing her arms around his neck. Steve reciprocated with a friendly kiss but kept an arm tightly round Alison. She no longer minded. She was looking forward to when the two of them could be by themselves, she didn't mind sharing him now.

The noise grew as the party got seriously under way, and people began making plans to eat, and at which restaurant, then Steve was explaining to her about the stag party he had been invited to that evening.

'Silly blighter's getting married.' The lines on his face were relaxed, his eyes laughing, and yet the words killed the happiness in her. She looked away from his face, murmuring something feeble, and shortly after, slipped away. How quickly the doubts came back—would she ever be free of them? If only she could enjoy a friendship with him, a love affair, and not take it too seriously.

But what was the use in thinking she could, when she couldn't bear the thought of living without him? She loved him more than anything. Without him she was nothing. But these were the things you didn't tell a man. You waited and waited for him to say them. How was it, Alison wondered, that some women could drop a hint and get him to say what she wanted to hear? She couldn't. When he was near her, it was like being caught in a gale, she was blown all over the place and incapable of rational thought, let alone able to say something planned.

'How is that area healing up on Ee-Wyn's tummy?' Steve, looking as if the stag party had gone on all night and he with it, reached a long arm for the treatment charts. Alison set down the tot she had in her arms and the child immediately opened its mouth to suck in enough air for a satisfactory scream. As Steve winced, Alison snatched him back up into her arms. 'There, there,' she said automatically. 'It's fine really,' she answered Steve.

'What is?' He frowned irritably. 'Does he have to make so much noise?' Alison signalled to Hine to come over and take the child. Before popping him into the nurse's arms she blew his nose with a tissue.

'I've got all the beds to change,' Hine complained as a tidal wave of sound engulfed them. Alison suddenly began to doubt the wisdom of dispensing with her uniform. Surely the nurses spoke back more often, the children were noisier.

'Never mind the confounded beds,' she said through gritted teeth. 'See if you can settle this little one down and the others might stop crying.' It was true. One started and then they were all bawling in sympathy. It was one of those mornings.

'Alison, can we get on? I do have an outpatients' clinic this morning. Did you take down Ee-Wyn's dressing yesterday?'

'Yes, we did,' Alison snapped back before she could help herself. She had little sympathy for people nursing a hangover when the ward was crammed with squalling kids and the nurses were turning Bolshie. 'I said it's fine. The area on her tummy, it's fine.'

'Good. Then that just leaves the buttocks. When she can lie comfortably on her front, we'll do a skin graft on her backside. No doubt you'll be able to talk the engineers into manufacturing some kind of apparatus that will help.'

'No doubt.' Suddenly and harshly they were bickering,

Alison frowning and Steve standing with his hands clasped ominously behind his back. What a noise there was! Why couldn't she go and order the children to be quiet and insist they stop racing their trucks down the passageways like any good Ward Sister?

'They're all so well, I should send the lot home,' Steve commented as he watched two small girls skipping past in their long cotton dressing gowns.

'That lot haven't had their tonsils out yet,' Alison reminded him drily. Catching a gleam of humour in the blue eyes, she smiled. Though for what reason, she couldn't think. 'Come into the office where it's quiet. I have a pot of fresh coffee on the desk.' He threw her a grateful look and followed meekly on her heels.

In the quiet cool room, she watched him gather up his long legs and sit down on the ridiculously low chair. He was far more comfortable sitting on her desk. While she was about it she served up two aspirin, along with a couple of sandwiches, suspecting he had gone without breakfast. Then she poured the coffee.

'Thanks, love,' his face split into a grin. 'From tomorrow I'll be the perfect consultant—promise.'

'I hope not,' she said with a sudden downturn of her beautiful mouth. 'Anyway, I'm really only trying to soften you up before breaking the bad news. Rosa's plaster is wet,' Steve's jaw dropped.

'We only got through changing it. When did this happen?'

'During the night. Chris is off sick and we had a relief.' Alison sighed. 'I know, I know. I did a few chartwheels myself. But it's soaked and it'll have to be changed again.' Steve spent a long time staring into his coffee while Alison waited.

'OK, the plaster needs changing,' he said quietly. She breathed in a sigh of relief. It was the sort of news that could send a doctor into orbit. It wasn't the wasted hours, the extra time spent trying to re-schedule a place in theatre or the long tedious job of getting the cast just right—but because it meant yet another trip to theatre for Rosa—an event they wanted to keep to the minimum. An unnecessary trip all because a nurse let the child sit in a pool of urine. It was inexcusable. Alison had come close to shaking the girl, but what was the use? She only did the odd night to supplement the family income and the hospital was so short of nurses it accepted anyone with a licence and game enough to come on to a strange ward and take charge of thirty-odd children.

'We've got to get something done about the staffing levels at night,' Alison said grimly.

'But I thought we had several mums come in during the night hours?'

Alison raised her eyebrows and stared at him.

'Yes, but they don't actually help with nursing duties. Chris says they spend most of the time in the kitchen drinking tea and talking. But then if their child is asleep what else are they to do? I don't know, I'm going to have to sort this business out. I mean, OK, it's an excellent idea, but we must have some control over the situation or I can see it getting out of hand. To say nothing of the children who don't get visits. And there are some, more than you'd think. They fret when the others have family constantly at their bed.'

'Why don't we allocate some time to get this sorted out?' Steve suggested. 'Maybe we can come up with a workable plan that falls somewhere in between. I've never known one yet that will please everyone, but we can try. And I'll back you with Matron for more night staff.' The top button of her blouse was undone, her nose was peeling and a long strand of hair had worked its way loose to tumble down her back; Steve searched back in his memory for the straight brisk little figure in the severe white starched veil who had ticked him off for touching the intravenous line, and he smiled, his eyes very blue as he regarded her.

'I'm sure we can find a compromise,' Alison was saying,

'but there is one other thing before you go. I saw Rangi's father yesterday,' she shrugged, something Steve noticed she did when upset, 'I didn't get very far with him, I'm afraid.'

'I gathered as much,' His mouth twitched with amusement. 'Last night I had a drink with the old man at the pub, and to cut a long story short, Rangi can go to your precious camp. I might add that I had to stand all his friends a round, and I hope you know how much that cost me.' Steve put his coffee cup on the table and stood up, rubbed his nose reflectively, gave her one of his vague sleepy smiles and was gone.

Alison collapsed back in her chair, arms draped over the sides and head falling backwards. Just like that, she mused, a drink with the lads and Rangi gets to go to camp.

'Oh, Alison . . .' She sat up with a jerk as Steve leaned back into the room. 'Thanks for the coffee and sustenance. If you're free this evening, I'd like to take you for dinner . . . And I thought you ought to know one of the hospital cats just gave birth in the linen room.'

Alison lost no time in getting to the linen room where an admiring assembly had gathered to witness the miracle while Sheba lay proudly on top of a pile of pristine white cot covers, oblivious to the fuss. Alison gave up asking how she got in there in the first place and was soon lifting children up so they might get a better view of the kittens. Hine arrived with a big cardboard carton.

'Good,' Alison approved. 'We can't leave her there, however sweet she looks. Oh, but Hine, not the coverlet, I have to account for every one.' Hine looked shocked.

'She can't be moved off just yet, Sister. She'll get upset and leave her kittens.' They all looked at Sheba, who did look as though she might decamp. Alison didn't want to be responsible for a family of orphans.

'Leave her be and put her somewhere quiet. But Hine, I want that coverlet back and sent to the laundry the very

first opportunity, understand?'
    'Yes, Sister.'

CHAPTER TEN

ALISON laid a hand on the girl's forehead, noticing the slight dampness with a frown. The pallor, too, was more extreme than in most children recovering from a routine, run-of-the-mill tonsillectomy. Her fingers went automatically to the carotid artery in the child's neck. 'Pulse seems normal,' she muttered, yet nagged by a sixth sense. 'How long has she been restless, Molly?'

'Only for the past few minutes, Sister. She's been fine.' The nurse's tone was persuasive. All post-operative tonsils were restless. It was Molly's considered opinion that Sister was fussing unnecessarily.

'It's that one case in a thousand,' Alison muttered, her eyes on the child's face. Molly was admiring the charts she had taken a lot of trouble over—red for the pulse, blue for respiration, blood pressure recorded in neat dotted lines with artful little arrowheads—Alison glancing up, observed drily, 'Charts are a useful guideline. They're not infallible, however. Remember, always look at your patient, Molly.'

'Yes, Sister.' Molly invested her voice with heavy patience. Honestly, there was nothing wrong with the kid. She was thankful to have her, at least she was still sleepy, unlike the two just come back from theatre and who were raising the roof. Why didn't Sister go see them, if she was so keen? Molly's eyes strayed to the window, she wondered what to give her dad for his birthday. It was always difficult thinking up what to give him. He had everything, didn't smoke . . .

'She's swallowing,' Alison said quietly.

'Huh . . .' Molly's eyes swivelled back to her patient.

'I don't like it. I'm going to notify the surgeon. If she's going to haemorrhage, it's within the first four hours and

169

now is the time. Let's get her over a bit.' With practised skill, Alison eased her young patient back into a lateral position and then went to the foot of the bed.

'I'll lift, you shove the blocks under.' Molly was dithering like a wet hen. 'Bottom cupboard,' Alison said, with a sharp nod in that direction. What wouldn't she give for several modern adjustable recovery beds! She heaved the end up as Molly came staggering over.

'Watch her closely in case she vomits,' Alison said—once the blocks were under the castors and the foot of the bed elevated—and left a shaken nurse.

'Hi . . . whoa there!' Steve caught up with her in the corridor. 'What's the rush?'

'Oh . . .' Alison's smile was brief, 'I was just going to call you. I don't like the look of little Amy Johnson—second on your list this morning—she's very sleepy still, a bit sweaty, and she's beginning to swallow too frequently.'

'Let's take a look.' Starting for the room, Steve observed, 'Funny, I thought at the time that kid might be a bleeder.' Molly was intensely relieved to see them, and moved aside. Steve looked sharply at Amy. A slight oozing of pink saliva showed at the corners of her mouth. He took the chart from Molly's unsteady hand and narrowed his eyes, his fingers firmly on the carotid pulse. 'She's bleeding all right. We'll have to ligate the vessel. Alison, ring theatre, tell them we're coming back.'

Alison was on her way even before he had stopped speaking. She grabbed Jenny Duncan in the corridor. 'Get the portable suction and go with Amy Johnson to theatre. Hurry! She's haemorrhaging.'

They had already gone, pushing Amy in her bed, by the time she was off the phone. The next hour dragged for Alison, though it wasn't for lack of things to do. Any operation could be dangerous, but this one particularly so. Amy could vomit the blood she had swallowed. It could be inhaled into her lungs. Had they been in time? These thoughts and similar preyed on her mind as she went about her work. When she saw Steve's tall figure at the end of the ward, she hurried to meet him. He was smiling.

'Amy's in recovery, a unit or two of blood and she'll be right as rain. We got her in the nick of time.' Alison closed her eyes briefly, thankfully.

'I was so afraid she'd vomit under the anaesthetic . . .' They talked quietly together, walking side by side along the corridor. At the office Steve's hand reached out to guide her in, the light touch on her wrist corroding her will-power.

She had decided, hadn't she, there could never be a second time for her. Let James be her first and last, her one big mistake. She didn't need to make another.

Last night at dinner, Steve had been wonderful, at ease, charming her into telling him her life story. God only knew, the charm of that man to bring people out of themselves, and get them to talk. How she had talked! Then she had sat opposite, the candle flickering between them, listening while he talked about himself, only now she detected a distance, and realised it had always been there. But she waited, certain he would tell her about his sister.

He hadn't. Not a word, and she hadn't asked. If she didn't know better, she wouldn't know he had one. Alison stood miserably in the office. How could she be close to someone who kept such an important part of his life secret? If he was capable of that, what might he not keep from her? And then he only had to touch her and she was telling herself that it didn't matter, that he could keep his secret.

But it did matter. After the dinner she had gone home and fallen face down on her bed wondering why she couldn't learn from her mistakes—the signs were there, she only had to look—to see that her dreams were only that. Dreams.

There was a knock at the door and Molly came in, her painted little face hovering above a loaded tea tray. 'Nurse, you're wonderful,' Steve said warmly, having noted the pile of sandwiches. Molly blushed and simpered, fully intending, obviously, to accept his gratitude and prepared

to forget her initial reluctance at being detailed to the
kitchen by Alison to make them.

'How's Amy?' Molly asked, shamelessly batting her
lashes—a curious shade of dark blue. Steve grinned and
took the tray from her and told her exactly how Amy was
and what they had done in theatre. When Molly had run
out of questions and had at last withdrawn, he sat down and
helped himself to the coffee Alison had poured. Alison
fiddled with the report. All she had to do was ask him. Why
did she find that so embarrassing? A simple question: I hear
you have a sister. Or: I saw you at the beach the other day.
Was that your sister with you? Something casual.

But instead, she opened her mouth and said, 'Aunt May's
invited us to dinner Friday night.' Steve reached a long
elegant hand for another sandwich. He thought how
adorable Alison looked when she was uncertain about
something, a hesitancy about her, eyes absorbed with
whatever it was on her mind. He longed to take her into his
arms and unwind the skein of silky hair and kiss her until
the pulse throbbed in her throat and her arms curled tightly
around his neck. God, how he wanted to kiss her!

'You don't seem very keen,' Alison said, mistaking the
long pause for a certain reluctance on his part.

'What . . . Oh, sorry. No, I was thinking of something
else,' he said wryly, resisting the impulse to tell her what
had been on his mind; though he loved to watch her
expression, the look of soft chastisement when he
murmured such things to her on the ward when he caught
her in a quiet moment. He grinned. 'Love to,' he said.

'Alison . . .' May detached herself from a small crowd of
shoppers and hurried to where Alison stood toying with a
selection of birthday cards, none of which seemed entirely
suitable for an elderly relative living a slender existence in
England.

May was excited. After a warm exchange of greetings she
pulled the wrappings from a carton and showed off its

contents. Alison counted at least one dozen crystal goblets, then glanced up. 'I'm planning something quite special for you two tomorrow night,' May told her. 'I was thinking how shabby my dinner ware was looking, and one thing led to another.'

'Oh, but Aunty—' Alison said, suddenly uneasy as May opened a large bag and produced a set of table linen, 'Aunty, I didn't want you to go to all this trouble . . .'

'It's no touble, love. It's about time we put on something for you and Steve. Henry suggested lamb, but I said not on your life. We're going to have duck and we'll start with a fish course.' May went on to tell Alison about the pâté she had made herself from three different varieties of fish; Alison took the carton and walked to the car with her. 'Sue-Ann's got a new dress with the money she saved. She's dying to show it off. Now, if I can only get Henry into a dinner jacket . . .'

'But Aunty,' Alison protested gently, 'we're not expecting anything like this. I thought it was going to be a simple family meal. I had no idea you were planning a big occasion.'

'Why not? It's not every day we welcome your young man to the family.' Alison was left staring blankly. How could she explain that that was just what she didn't want, because there was hardly a chance of it ever happening. 'I'm praying my crême brulée is a success,' May chattered happily. 'Henry said to make an apple pie. He thinks all men like apple pies. Oh, now don't you go and worry yourself. I like doing it. He's special, that man of yours. I knew it the moment I first saw him. No, I said to Henry, he'll appreciate my crême brulée.' Alison couldn't help a smile. If he appreciated the delicate texture and subtle flavours of her famous dessert, then he was one man in a million. The two went together in May's estimation of things. Despite her doubts, she began to feel the potent mixture of excitement and apprehension rock climbers must experience nearing the end of a dangerous climb.

Steve was special. He must be, to have captured her soul, made her run into his arms, his strong gentle passionate arms—when all along she knew the foolishness of getting involved with a man who couldn't walk down a hospital corridor without attracting the attention of every nurse within range. Who had, moreover, the personality of a hexagon, and who kept half the facets hidden so that she never really knew what he was thinking, or feeling. Who was so diffident about his own private life, she knew practically nothing of importance about it, other than what came up in the course of the day. But who had stripped the hard protective covers from her until her soft inner core was exposed, until he made her feel like a woman again, soft, vulnerable, yet at the same time strong and vibrant, exciting, sensuous.

In a flash of something akin to terror, Alison knew she would never be able to walk away from him with her heart and reason intact. Never. There was no choice. She had, without knowing it, lost her autonomy, was no longer free. She must try this one last time, and if that didn't work out, she would have to go back to England. Leave while she still had her dignity, for how could she bear seeing Steve every day knowing she had been only one in a long, long line?

She left May smiling happily and hurried homewards. What was it about the magic of love that gave her feet wings, that made all things seem possible and caused her to smile at every passer-by? Quoting Robert Browning, 'Oh lyric love, half angel and half bird. And all a wonder and a wild desire . . .' she forgot that love was also, always, fearful and apprehensive, and she woke to her alarm bell the next morning with a nameless dread. A feeling she could not thrust aside until her attention was claimed by the controlled hysteria of operating day on a children's ward.

Alison replaced the phone and hurried out into the corridor, her bottom lip caught between her teeth. 'Staff Nurse Duncan around?' she asked, pushing open the treatment room door. 'Oh, Jenny, thank goodness! Clair's stuck with a patient in X-Ray. I'll have to get you to see to Ee-Wyn. She should be ready to go to theatre, if you could just check her over, please.' At Jenny's nod, Alison withdrew and was about to hurry away, when a sudden premonition prompted a reminder.

'Remember,' she said, thrusting her head back round the door, 'two sites have got to be prepared for her skin graft—doner and recipient.' Jenny was in the act of drawing up an antibiotic solution and she nodded vaguely. Alison was in two minds to check Ee-Wyn out herself, and was just about to when the phone called her back to her office. In any case, what was the fussing about? Both Clair and Jenny knew what they were doing, they wouldn't slip up on an important point like that.

Alison had seen Steve when he did a quick round before surgery. He had seemed preoccupied, but, she thought, undertandably so considering the list he had in front of him. Alison knew too that he would worry about Ee-Wyn until she was safely back in the ward. Then, she thought, with a wry smile, he would worry about her until the graft took. Alison's brow puckered into a frown. With Clair leaving to go to Australia soon, who would take over the care of Ee-Wyn during the vital days when the grafted tissue was at its most vulnerable. Jenny? And could she spare her from the ward where her valuable experience was of such importance? With these thoughts on her mind, the morning slipped away like so much quicksilver.

She was surprised when Steve put in an appearance late morning, with his white coat pulled on over his theatre greens. 'You're not cancelling the rest of the list?' she asked, sensing something was wrong by the expression on his face. Then as a sudden fear took hold of her, she asked, 'Ee-Wyn? Nothing's happened?'

'Ee-Wyn is fine, she's along in recovery.' The blue eyes were trained on her now. 'We got off to a late start because my scrub nurse had to prepare the second site and then glove up again. You might remind whoever was responsible for preparing Ee-Wyn for surgery of that fact.' Alison bit her lip and moved aside to allow a recovery trolley go past, then they moved on down the ward, Steve stepping over a dump truck with the ease of a practised hurdler.

'Jimmy, take it outside, please,' she said, more sharply than she intended. It wasn't the dump truck on her mind. 'I'm terribly sorry,' she said to Steve 'Of course I'll look into it, but I should have checked myself.'

'Forget it,' Steve said tersely. 'You can't be expected to be everywhere at once. Look, Alison . . .' he stopped, and she turned so they were face to face in the sunlight spilling in from the open doors. Alison didn't speak, perhaps because she had a sense of what was coming.

'Alison, the list is going to run on into the afternoon, then I've got a clinic. I can't see me finishing up here until six at the earliest, and honestly, I think the best thing is to drop out of tonight's arrangement, if we can.'

Alison shook her head, wide-eyed. 'We can't. Steve, you have no idea the preparations May's made . . .' He was frowning.

'But you said it was going to be just a family meal and if we felt like joining them, or something to that effect.' He bent to pick up the child clinging to his leg while Alison automatically pulled a tissue from her pocket. 'Blow, Riti—that's it. I know,' she said, looking up at Steve, 'that's what I thought, I had no idea she was going to a lot of trouble . . .' her voice faded as she stood with her eyes fixed on his face. 'May said seven . . . We'd have time.' He looked so tired. But what could she do? She couldn't ring May and cancel now.

'Seven it is then,' Steve said, and though she was relieved, his forced smile did nothing to raise her spirits. 'And if that's the case, I'd better get weaving.' He popped Riti into her arms with a lift of his dark brows and off he went. She watched him stride down the ward and disappear along the corridor with the sad sort of foreboding she had woken with returning.

From then on, the day was all downhill. Stuart went on his half day forgetting to chart the post-operative medications and Rob couldn't be reached for fully an hour because his bleeper was defective. Two nurses became ill and Alison worried herself into a headache thinking the children would all come down with a stomach bug; but then the complaint was diagnosed as food poisoning and traced to some shellfish soup eaten by the nurses in town. By the time six o'clock was approaching Alison felt dirty and sticky and would have given anything for a shower. But she would have had to go over to the Nurses' Home, and there simply wasn't time.

She made do with a good wash along in the small changing room at the end of the ward, then pulled the silk shirt from its hanger and grimaced. If she were to look pale and interesting, it would be fine. But not with the high colour she had acquired over a hectic afternoon. Bright cerise pink had been a bad choice. Slipping into a straight black skirt, she peered anxiously in the mirror and sighed with dismay. She might be going to the office. Early that morning she had thought the combination would be chic.

'And her hair was a mess. She had washed it last thing the night before and slept on it damp, and it wouldn't go right. She groaned, the corners of her mouth drooping as she looked at herself. She looked more like thirty-five than only just thirty. And Steve—she winced—Steve always looked a boyish twenty.

'Ah, there you are.' Steve was prowling along the corridor with the hunted look of a man trapped into something against his will. Alison almost wished that she herself had been dealt a dose of suspect food—then she could have legitimately called the evening off (promising even then to be a disaster) and gone home and buried herself in bed, and everyone would have been sympathetic and Steve could take that hounded look off his face. He was, as she expected he would be, looking outrageously young and handsome in his delictable navy blazer, crisp white shirt and striped tie, impeccable trousers pressed and creased to a knife edge.

'Little one's recovering well,' observed Steve as they marched along the corridors. Alison nodded. He meant Ee-Wyn. He often called her the little one.

'Yes,' she agreed, 'doing splendidly.' Did she imagine he was giving her a strange look? As well he might, if she looked as much a wreck as she felt.

Trying rather desperately to cover a mood of utter dejection, Alison kept up an incessant line of small talk all the way out to the farm. The more she chattered, she noticed, the more quiet and withdrawn Steve appeared. What little he had to say had to do with Clair's imminent departure.

He still cares about her, thought Alison, unhappily turning her face to the window on her side and winding the expensive silk handkerchief—which should have been fluttering from her breast pocket—around and around her fingers. Steve brought the Land Rover to an abrupt stop at the farm gate and she stumbled out to open it, catching her high heels in the cattle stop.

'Why bother with a gate when you have a cattle stop?' Steve muttered as she climbed back in. He sounded irritable, and she shrugged.

'Perhaps the sheep are able to get out along the side of the thing,' she ventured, her eyes turned studiously away from him.

'Cattle stops are built to prevent that happening,' Steve said, reducing her to a brooding silence. He rammed the stick into low gear and they started up the rutted road to the farmhouse.

Sitting numbly in one of the uncomfortable, straight-backed dining room chairs, Alison watched Henry work with energy and precision over the duck, while May, dressed in electric blue chiffon, handed out plates and a patter of small talk with the dispatch of the possessed.

Sue-Ann, who had been chastised before their arrival for dripping redcurrant sauce on to the new linen tablecloth, looked sulky. And Steve, Alison decided, merely looked bored. In a more charitable mood she might have thought he was bemused, but she was steadily convincing herself she was beginning to know him a lot better. At the moment he was listening to May with a frozen look of polite interest.

Finished at last with his carving, Henry picked up a wine glass and delivered a little speech of welcome. It sounded hideously like the sort of speech a father would make for a potential son-in-law; an impression Steve must also have gained, Alison surmised, from the look of his raised brows.

Why couldn't they just be their nice homely normal selves? she thought, cringing at how stiff and pretentious Steve would see them as. She wished her uncle wouldn't keep addressing him as, 'my boy', or dwell on the fact that Steve had known her father in London. Steve wouldn't want to be reminded of that.

'Sue-Ann,' Steve said, after the pleasantries had flown around the table, 'any more thoughts about a nursing career?'

Sue-Ann speared a potato with her knife and caused May's fork to waver in mid-air.

'Thought about it,' Sue-Ann claimed, 'but I dunno. I don't want to spend my life lugging bedpans about. I want to be an air hostess.' This seemed news to her parents and for a while, there was a spirited exchange of views, until Sue-Ann asked if she might be able to join her brothers—who had apparently been excused the necessity of attending the dinner party and who were now enjoying a beach barbecue.

May looked doubtful, but Henry said genially, 'Run along, I'm sure Alison and Steve won't mind. Be back by eleven, though.' After Sue-Ann's departure he turned to Steve and poured more wine, proceeding with a discourse on the family history, May eagerly adding the details.

Steve sat quietly, nodding here and there and occasionally

laughing, forced, Alison supposed, into putting on some kind of show. After watching him covertly she could tell he wasn't interested. The lines of his face were rather too compressed, his eyes hooded and at variance with the general air of relaxation. He was bored, she thought. Bored at having been made to spend an evening in the company of her relatives. And quite likely he was bored with her.

It wouldn't surprise her. She was no great catch for a man like Steve, Alison persuaded herself, shedding illusions in an agony of weariness. Perhaps he only desired the unobtainable—now that Clair was actually leaving, he wanted her.

Her heart ached when she thought of how hard her aunt had worked to try and make the evening a success. Even if the ambitious plans had become a bit unstuck, she somehow suspected Steve might have appreciated her family even less had the meal been the usual homely affair at the big kitchen table with the boys talking nineteen to the dozen and jostling Sue-Ann, May flustered and red-faced from the stove and Henry comfortable in old slippers and baggy pullover. She looked away, and was startled when Steve reached over and touched her wrist.

'You're very quiet tonight?' Alison steadied the trembling his touch never failed to produce, while marvelling that even now, even now, she was ready to ignore the obvious and succumb. That was how far gone she was. Thank God, when all this was over, she had the dignity and continuity of work to immerse herself in. Except that while his hand still lay on her wrist, she could only think of him as the man she loved.

'We must be going,' he said quietly, and she felt his hand leave her wrist, though the impression remained. 'It's late and we're both very tired.' Charmingly he turned down another portion of May's crême brulée, claiming he had never tasted anything more exquisite. They stood up from the table. While he was having a last few words with Henry, Alison asked her aunt quietly if she might stay the night, explaining that she was off duty the next day, and of course, May was delighted at the prospect of her company.

'Coming, Alison?' Steve grasped her hand and drew her after him, turning to wave from the bottom step. The night air was crisp and she shivered. 'Haven't you a coat or jacket?' he asked, glancing at her as they walked to the gate. She withdrew her hand.

'I didn't think to bring anything. Anyway . . .' she paused, her heart heaving about inside her. But she knew what she had to do. She had to end it. Better now than drag it on until he was the one forced to. 'Steve . . .' She leaned up against the Land Rover, feeling as though her knees were going to give out on her.

'Can't we talk on the way home?' He stood beside her, becoming taller and larger and more of a riddle to her than ever. An enigma of a man whose innermost thoughts were still a mystery to her. Yet she had never been so aware of him.

'I won't be coming back with you,' she said, trying hopelessly to control a tremor in her voice and avoid his eyes. She mustn't look at his face. He was too close to her, and she moved away a little, pressing her hands tightly together, aware of his puzzled look. Hastily and fearfully she turned to speak before he did some tender kind thing that would have her melting into his arms.

'I think it best if I stay here at the farm the next two days. You see, my dear . . .' Just for a second she faltered, the deadly realisation of what she was doing all but drying up her voice. She forced herself on, convinced it was what he wanted to hear. Convinced it was futile to think she could be the woman he wanted at his side for life. He was young, in no hurry to be tied down. There would be no shortage of lovely young things ready to fall into his bed on his terms and willing to play the game any way he wanted. Whereas she had never learned the trick of taking a love affair lightly.

'. . . I think that perhaps we're getting too involved with each other . . .' She was the one who was too involved.

'What are you trying to say? His voice had never been so stern, and how grateful she was for the darkness that shielded his face from hers.

'I suppose that what I'm trying to tell you is that I feel we're not suited, and that I think we should call it a day.' Alison felt she had started on a hazardous journey and that she would never get to the end. She forced a little laugh through her stiff lips. 'Better to find out now than later, don't you think?'

It wasn't what she thought, at all, but it seemed the simplest excuse. She was sure he would appreciate being let off the hook so easily. No tears, no recriminations.

'I see,' he said quietly, nodding. Was that all? Alison clenched her hands waiting for him to say something else. How much more could she endure of his watching her in silence, assessing, annotating? She heard his sigh as he raked a hand through his hair in a gesture she had come to know. Well, no man liked being given the push, she thought. It was something he preferred to do himself.

'Well . . .' She rubbed at her arms and said something about it being cold and that she should be going in and wished him a safe trip back to town, managing it in a light chatty tone of voice; when all she wanted was to rush into his arms and hide herself against that big strong body. While she was still able, she said goodbye, turned, and walked quickly back up the path to the lamplit porch.

The end of a love affair is always sad and painful, to Alison, staring unseeing at the television in the stultifying normalcy of her aunt's sitting room, it was as if her life had gone, swirling away as chaff in the wind. She longed to escape to her bedroom and solitude. Nevertheless she waited, the milk drink growing cold in her hands. It was expected of her to sit the customary hour before going up. Anything else would be unusual. She didn't want that. She didn't want to rouse any suspicion that all was not well. Sympathy now would unnerve her, totally.

'That young man of yours,' Uncle Henry took his pipe in his hand and leaned companionably in her direction, 'I like him very much. Very much.' A twitch of appreciation on his mouth, he settled himself back and resumed a reflective puffing. May smiled over her knitting.

In a moment of deathly quiet, Alison saw what she had done. Her happiness had hung by one tenuous thread; oblivious to the frightful results, she had snapped it. The reasons that felt justifiable at the time seemed oddly misplaced now. Panic began to rise, until she felt she would suffocate in its stranglehold. Thoughts, recollections, memories, began slipping back and forth in her mind. Each held a little of Steve; without him the years ahead stretched in an uninterrupted line, an interminable desert.

Carefully she put down the mug on the little table by her side. She needed a great gulp of cold fresh air to steady her. Seek to ease her discomfort in a long exhausting walk. Find some place where she could cry and not be overheard.

'Put my cardigan over your shoulders, it's turned nippy,' May advised, looking over her spectacles.

Fingers trembling, Alison hurriedly took the thick yellow garment and pulled it around her shoulders without a thought to the hideous combination of mustard and cerise pink. Who cared what she looked like? She let herself out the front door and down the porch steps, clutching the cardigan at the neck, hair flying in the wind, her feet thrust into a pair of May's old slippers. Down the uneven brick path, past the spent delphiniums and the autumn-tinged hydrangea to the gate, and there, without any warning, she found Steve settled comfortably against the high box hedge.

She was frozen in her tracks. She couldn't think. Words kept beating in her brain, they made no sense. Yet there he was, six feet away from her, lounging back with his hands in his pockets, the same lazy smile. Quite forgetting to breathe, she let out a gasp of pulverised air.

'What are you doing here?' she asked, not even mindful to be delicate.

'Waiting for you.' Steve was grinning broadly. 'Thought you might come out for a breath of air.' He straightened up from his nest in the tough springy foliage and came forward until he was right beside her.

'Alison . . .' It was all he said. He was looking down at her and she was in his eyes. She couldn't rescue herself. She stood waiting. Then he reached for her, pulling her into the sanctuary of his arms. For a long aching moment they stood entwined, heartbeat to heartbeat, his protecting warmth driving the winter from her soul.

Quite slowly he cupped her chin, raising her face to his, her eyes enormous, her skin translucent as the moon slid behind a cloud; then his lips found her mouth and her arms were about his neck as though she never intended to be parted from him. He kissed her again and again, until her mind reeled and slipped through a violent radiance. When at last he drew back his head, he held her closely, his arms tight about her.

'I thought you'd gone,' she wept, one tear after the other running boiling hot down her face.

'You'll have to try harder than that to get rid of me.' His voice was dark and sad. 'You're shivering,' he said, and undid the buttons of his jacket and pulled her inside, nestling her against his body. His possessive hands stroked and hugged and caressed. Raindrops spattered over them as a sudden squall blew up, and still they didn't move.

'Why?' he asked her, his voice husky. 'Why did you do it? All this confounded rot about not being suited. You know as well as I do, it's a load of rubbish.'

Before reason deserted her completely, she had to try and explain the yawning uncertainty that made her do it. She told him about the day she had seen him on the beach and about her suspicion that it was Kirstin he was with. And when that was cleared up, her misery and sadness that he had not confided in her. And because he hadn't, she thought she meant so little to him.

Steve wiped her tears away with a soft linen handkerchief.

'You think that was it,' he said, enfolding her in his arms once more and rocking her gently to and fro. 'But it's not the real reason that made you run for cover.' He looked down at her. 'You were scared to trust another man. You wanted out, before there was any chance you might be rejected again.'

The truth hurt. But she knew it to be the truth. Even with her marvellous capacity for obliterating the past, she had managed to drag the old hurt and wounded pride with her to ruin another relationship, the most important one of her life.

Steve looked beyond her into the darkness of the night and his voice was charged with such feeling, Alison looked up. 'I should have told you, long ago. God knows, I wanted to. Trish . . .' in the small silence, she felt the ache behind his sister's name, 'Trish refused to see anyone at first. She couldn't bear to think of herself as a cripple, let alone be seen. Then one day she agreed to a visit, and gradually she got to trust me. She hated the thought of being talked about, and particularly that I was discussing her behind her back. She became paranoid about it and in the end, I had to promise I wouldn't. I kept that promise, knowing it to be quite irrational, silly even. When we were kids, she always knew when I'd betrayed a promise, she said she could read the guilt on my face.' His eyes met hers. Clear, steady, unwavering eyes. This was no man with a glib explanation , this was someone who had suffered and who was sincere.

'I love you,' he said, with an astonishing shyness. 'And I want to marry you.' Rain dripped from his chin, each drop Alison would remember for the rest of her life, and then she was crying again, her own salt tears mingling with the rain, and nodding, not able to say a thing.

'Well?' he demanded. 'Will you or won't you?' In his impassioned embrace it was almost impossible to draw breath.

'Oh, Steve, I love you . . .' And as his arms threatened to squeeze the life out of her she gasped, 'I will. I will marry you.' As she spoke, a peal of thunder rolled through the heavens. She looked up into his face, laughing as the rain came pelting down. 'You'll have to come on in and get dry by the fire.'

'Not until I've kissed you properly,' he said, hugging his bride-to-be. Alison grabbed his arm and led him to a small wooded gate in the hedge, where on the other side was the orchard, a dark tangle of trees they could shelter under.

He followed her through the wet grass until they reached an arbour formed by the thick vines of the passion-friut tree. The air was like wine and the stars, beginning to shine again, shone for them. As she turned to him he took her into his arms with such tenderness, Alison felt joy surge through her body. Tingling and alive, they clung to each other. He had her, and she wanted nothing else.

'And then he asked me to marry him,' Alison said, awe in her voice, after they had walked in from the rain, soaking wet and radiant, to be hustled to the fire by an anxious May. Alison looked lovingly at the man by her side. She might not know him very well yet, but it no longer mattered. She had a lifetime to find out. They loved each other. She had such happiness now, nothing that could ever happen would change the way she felt for him.

Henry put a mug of hot tea in her hands, not quite sure why Alison had sounded so surprised her young man wanted to marry her. He'd known at dinner that Steve was head over heels in love with her. Could have told her so. He went to answer the phone, leaving May to fuss endlessly about the details.

'It's all right, Mother,' he announced, coming back into the room. 'Sue-Ann and the boys are safe and sound. They're over at the McCullys'. Be home soon as they've had a hot drink, shouldn't wonder.'

'Steve,' Alison whispered, her face suddenly anxious, 'what about Trish? How will she take it?'

'Didn't I tell you?' he grinned. 'She knows all about you.

She said if there was going to be a wedding, she wants to come to it. She wouldn't do it, unless she thought I loved you more than life itself.'

Such joy, and she thought it could never be hers. All the times he had appeared on the ward, standing loftily on the other side of a patient's bed in his white coat; the times he had walked by her side, taken a howling child from her arms; all the tender, sweet moments he had accidently touched her arm and she had inadvertently encountered his eyes—all this, leading to now. Alison laid her head back on his shoulder within the protecting circle of his strong arm, and felt the corner of his chin come to rest gently on her head.

Mills & Boon present
the 75th Romance of one of their top authors

CHARLOTTE LAMB
NO MORE
LONELY NIGHTS

Charlotte Lamb's popularity speaks for itself. This intriguing and romantic story, tying together the hard high powered world of the business magnate with the softness of the human heart, is destined to become a collector's item.

Not to buy this title is to miss a classic.

Published: September 1988   Price £1.50

The latest blockbuster from Penny Jordan

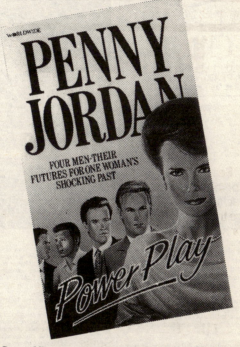

For Pepper Minesse, success as a young and powerful business woman has always been fuelled by one consuming desire – revenge against the 4 men involved in sadistically raping her in her teens.

Now she is ready.

She holds files that could destroy the lives and careers of these prominent men.

Together they must silence her – for ever.

Only one man's love can diffuse the insanity of the situation.

This blockbuster is Penny Jordan's most gripping and dramatic novel to date. Nothing can beat POWER PLAY

SPOT THE COUPLE
AND WIN A
£1,000
REAL PEARL NECKLACE
PLUS 10 PAIRS OF REAL PEARL EAR STUDS WORTH OVER £100 EACH

A

B

No piece of jewellery is more romantic than the soft glow and lustre of a real pearl necklace, pearls that grow mysteriously from a grain of sand to a jewel that has a romantic history that can be traced back to Cleopatra and beyond.

To enter just study Photograph A showing a young couple. Then look carefully at Photograph B showing the same section of the river. Decide where you think the couple are standing and mark their position with a cross in pen.

Complete the entry form below and mail your entry PLUS TWO OTHER "SPOT THE COUPLE" Competition Pages from June, July or August Mills and Boon paperbacks, to Spot the Couple, Mills and Boon Limited, Eton House, 18/24 Paradise Road, Richmond, Surrey, TW9 1SR, England. All entries must be received by December 31st 1988.

ENTRY FORM

Name _____

Address _____

_____

I bought this book in TOWN _____ COUNTRY _____

This offer applies only to books purchased outside the UK & Eire.
You may be mailed with other offers as a result of this application.